T0247394

solip

a novel • Ken Baumann

Tyrant Books
676A 9th Ave. #153
New York, New York 10036
nytyrantbooks.com

Cover and book design by Ken Baumann

•

for
Gian, Michael, Blake, Dennis, Chris, Mark, Eric, David,
Evan, Alec, Ignatius, Vicki, Bob, Aviva, Aviva,
Aviva.

The call of love sounds very hollow
among these immobile rocks.
—Gustav Mahler

Bending limbs in dark like this is only cautionary movement. Were I to lock up, creak to a slow, I would be nothing but a gravid caterpillar within my womb, self-entombed and shallow breath presumed. To die! My father spake of me with wet eyes on evenings salted cinnamon; the oven! The oven, he said. How he wished he could stick me in it.

There is a room.

Or to place myself in time: Years. A here. Ensconced. Within a stripping of skin. Within a way of asking.

And to time myself in place: A perception of me and limit of me is something I cannot grasp. I have not hands small enough.

More?

Games like memory and sense went gone years ago. I've grown bigger.

How those that have roaming space delimit that place until it's plainly a set of compartments to move through.

In a wide gutted prime there are corners, grime. Six planes or ways that stop. In a box. Room? I've felt only five. Room? A room as a well is the ocean.

There could be a roof. I can't reach. I've lobbed hand-fuls up, and no slap. Peering over the edge of the well, and dropping a stone, and never hearing water talk, this is speaking in here. Where I am. What I am, here. An always empty stomach, looping symbol. Loping cornered. Bound up because there is no door.

For I can and only motion for the body, its concerns. I speak now inside myself, receptor, in hopes it cepts and sends. Taking full working hours; the clock is a body that buries. Time is a body. (our boy) Time is a body in light.

I am in dark.

Prolonged corporeal twirls, optimistic arm-weaves, can sometimes get me to a euphoric plane, familiar to those who run past walls. Walls.

Had I cut my fingernails short at length day one, I

could've measured the width between our walls. The height above me, if I kept cutting and throwing on a burial mound, pyramid, pyre. I could've stripped and stacked, or laid end to end. Could've cut and bit and used to bit. I could've gone to prayer for every calliope.

We are not unlike, you and I.

A box, a box, a box, a box. Dark and walls, a box, a box.

Too human: Tumorous concerns, like a singing stomach or the severed proffered hand that often comes and goes. I'm bothered.

Can I go dumb if I refuse? Forget at all if I use? Talk not to stop ought. Rather bark. Sour tickling is confined: Base of the skull or summit of stem. It's very peculiar!

I want you here for a long time. I want you to know me.

Alright, goddamnit, back to it. Outside. Grab the ball. Turn around. Goddamnit. How long we're going to teach you is up to you, boy.

ECHO: We can stay here all day. (night)

Calisthenics, no form, grace given not gained. A morning sweat. Ritual. Ritual. Breath-phenom, a boy wonder. Contained Against His Will! Girl Cries Wolf, Sentenced to Eternal Room! May He Die? May We Die In Here Already?

If I condoned the formal use, I would recall and retell all the loss: The loss of my clothes to grabby hands, the hose, the bootstrap leather welts, the hair pulled and cut back in a jerk, scalp slit too, out of sloppiness, the subsequent graft and gown-wearing, the white walls instead of black walls. Black walls are the walls.

Black walls are the walls—

Fevered I achieve loops of it, glints of pain. Connect a welting to every breath. Proceed to breathe. The breathing forms the loop. The loop is a delirium, yes, but a stir worth starving for. Handling a large box swathed in a layer of foam, with just an inch of pin sticking out and into our chest, the pin pushing into our skin, and the box cannot be dropped. A handling and a breach. Every breath. Cannot, acone, not be contained. Vision: Every exhalation as smoke.

To those receiving: Please close my cell in. Close it in so my cells can swim.

FUZZ: Broadcast journalism at its finest, folks.

Imperceptible spider webs in the corners of the roof. Congregations of spiders. They meet where the walls meet. They meat everywhere but center. I stay there when I hear their webs billow. I don't need light to to keep—

A sweat fugue. Self-preservation is the state.

(god laughter)

And even though I haven't eaten from the hand I still feel I can go without breathing!

Transmission will be intermittently interrupted by sounds of sobbing. Pardon us. The sobbing is getting clearer. A nirvana among weeds.

Ethos of an era embodied by: Me! It is? That's it, the sound—Meee!—of a boiling lobster. I am that lobster. I can fake new limbs in any direction. Struck, I am! Stuck, he makes me. For each mark he makes, a soul he takes. Our father who art in Heaven, hallowed be thy name, uhh.

Rest?

To those listening: A map! A map will be done. A map I will map of my flesh; promises cannot be kept. Promises cannot be kept about content. Suffice it to say I will stay avarice. Because sometimes in this dark I'll forget parts. I've been conditioned so. My back will cease to be, simply. Suddenly I am half of me, dreading a half of back. Toes vanish. Maybe they go, or maybe they are misplaced. Either way, they reaffix when I stumble over them, upon them, onto them, as if they come and go again and again in yearning, magnetic or sticky. Phantoms.

To start with the skin: The cup runeth over, my dear. I'm encased in the stuff. A treatise on dust would be pertinent if I could see motes at all, but no, too dark. I am in my negative blanket fugue and must behave according-ly. But, need reminding: Dust is the stuff of the stuff of the body. Now grin.

Covered completely in myself, congregated, a mass of dilated pupils and shedding wares, supine. I often lie. (down) The floor must be pumped cool underneath by a machine of great quiet; the humming I can only hear once the ghost is gone, the fatherless hand, and I'm retrieved.

11

There may be noise. I do feel hummed. No good. Retract-
ed.

Made a promise? Redacted.

The webbing of my fingers is a great gloam of worry.
They'll be cut. They'll be cut, he say! Fsk fsk! The royal
birthmark, a scar truly, bloomed his right cheek and down
to his neck, under the shirt we suspected. The royal. A
man with glasses. We as children knew only to pass.
(hymn)

My head is down. My head is down. With complete
conviction now: My head is down.

Imagine a yellow plain. A breeze. Wheat makes the
sound. The plain, now, an oilfield. Thumping cyclic
pumps from the red hammers. The hammers gone. The
plain yellow with wheat, clean again. A spout of fire a
hundred feet high, burning oil. Men worry, to burn. The
great fire so great it catches the oil afire in the tubes; the
men run the field, run to a point in the tubes where the oil
hasn't stoked; can they beat the fire? Can they beat the fire?
They run for hours and reach stake and dig, dig and dig,
checkered soil mounds surround the men and their hole,
form loose pyramids. The men are the most tired they've
ever been, they could ever be. They labor through it.
Their bodies start to fail. The hole grows wider. They
jump in without planning a way out. Their shovels begin
to blunt.

Finally: Pipe.

The tallest man reaches up with his shovel and strikes down on the pipe and:

When asked, decline the radial censorship test. They will give it to you anyway.

Transmittable, not immutable.

(they burn)

Back to body! Body to body: Is the brain, a sponge, not body? I cannot stand for twenty-one grams. No, no, no. Ever looked inside the caverns inside? They are deep and bubbled with gastric pink. Cave ripples and slick. Dripping stalactites are thoracic rib spikes and spiking stalagmites are the veins of the feet. How the blood pools in the center. In the center, see? See him out there? Swimming. Water so blue it's black again. His breathing echoes through the lungs around him. He can only go, diving, so deep.

Plumbed.

In some slice of time, static and spark swells the air; my top skin feels lifted away from me; detached from the muscle, pulled outward and all at once. One inch out, a one inch expansion. An empty air between the separate skin.

I see myself back there—NO MEMORY—I often see myself—

Hovering. Stasis. I'm in the office of my tormentors. I'm in the box outside this box; the former leading to the latatatter. I'm stuck in the air, the office air amber and I am bug. Myself, a copy self, sits across from another: A man, himself. Glasses. Mustache. Pleasant enough in the Brown coat and White shirt and Red tie and, he first—

So.

So?

So.

Tubelike, sucked back out.

Here I am! Here I am, pappy! Back home. Puppy in tow.

Stop reenacting what's told?

Ocular trauma; a great Greek tragedy

Can we ever?

A Roman oratorio; a symphony of absence. The dark so long, and not oft punctuated, as to become impenetrable and all hanging, all framing. A heaven in the mist. The formless mirage. Forever. Until the hand.

NOW it opens into a white lotus, peels and fills, the hand, I only question the horrible chimes that come with it, once it moves, its fingers are more curling and make my jaw quake and then molars, I can only squeeze myself so shut, the hand unwinds as if unwillingly pried, I can only pray, there is a pale of it, its real, level to sight but even if I'm laid down its level is set right, above me, or beyond the floor, there is no space, as it uncurls, and is, a pale gravity, and the chiming is rapid or fades

I'm caused a space. Oops. Our first. Post fuzz.

I can't tell you how it goes away.

So to the soles of feet which are black. Surely, they must stain the whole floor with whatever it is that leaks. Seen it, surely. The black stains, pads and the heels, stain-ed. The grime that must be layered. Or.

Is it better/best to salt the wound before or after infection?
Before! After!

Others promise a transparency. A line. A vista of faith, shared by many. Men and women build a house that is recognizably unrecognizable. They live there. It leaks at the seams. Then what goes. They cry at night. We have to move forward. The scream. They are bewitched by hard light. What they do not know, those housed, is that light moves under what is gone.

A house, a home, a hovel. Hi. And in it this homily. There's clear up and wisps of information seeping. I can turn around, I can turn back and dive again. And if I do— we're diving. Stars in periphery. And now we're here, in the much feared void. Void. It is easy to say hello, because the void says hello right back. Try it, children! (hi) Continuing on. By now we've been crushed and folded within what is invisible, and that's fun, it's fun. We are left okay to sink, diving no longer an option; whence the laws move! They and we are begat. Travel onward takes an indeterminate amount of time, if you—we—I—can call it that. The suck is inessential and two-dimensional. We'll get there—KEEP IT DOWN BACK THERE—and, one cannot say for sure but one can feel: The nexus is as near as it can be with all known. Nexus. A plane of practice. Myth achieved.

Here: A royal bloom—

Spit out amongst, mass, and now the dust floats and bubbles, great storms, fire of heaven and clumps of iodine. Swollen with births. New cancer.

I can only light fire with my belly. Again: No promises.

Replication is nice, a goal, just feinted short of imperative, death drive. If I could, I can, when I break a piece of myself, it could plant, somehow I will plant it above ground, treat with water pooled in my naval, and watch it grow: To have fathered something impaternal. Impersonal only in the wheel of caves. Dark would let the child's love keep in his eyes. Perhaps, past the toddling stage, I could proffer him to the hand or the becoming, put him through the wall, swathed, gently push the light back.

A fair deal—an agreement—could then be struck. The hand could encore, to shake! From then: My oh my, a new era in cellkeep. I promise that. Even if the child grew and bared fruit: Layer paternis, daddy Genesis, would stay kempt. Mulch!

Your father not your father. His blood not your blood. Your father is a stranger; his blood to know, alone. Your mother is here so hear your mother: Your heart will not seize. Your family is a brick. Your body now a salt, eroded. Your family is a blood, your family is a run like walls.

I was told—

Omission.

I think enough about a scaffold and a rope and my head becomes them. Designing, building. Curving interiors rid of dust; splits and spits. Maybe now I build the platform. Supposedly they start from the ascent:

Boots on the wood, a curling coat from years of no use. Slow approach. The hand on my left arm. A footstep on the first step heard and I take it. Up a number more than four and they stretch, maybe along the guard's upping rhythm I must to follow. Maybe a gum chewed and a verse between them, the guards. Two or three and a priest. He takes me up on flat ground. It's a plateau. One of more. I can see from it. My breathing hot and clean and moving away too soon out of the black cloth. I am up here, a head almost cut and cast sliding on the smoothest air. Heavy feet, they say. Laughing would echo and find tracks to clap in the big space holding all. Seen pictures. Warehouse hanging; not the act but the place in time. I am being served, we are all serving, and there's our community. A prophet started saying or keeping me seconds ago. What if my sides split open and pour forth? The guards could bathe in it. If I've given it to you, you could uncap me and all you'd see is a little gallows.

Open and sick and blinking so much so, or in which you feel your blood slick through your legs and pool in your toes. This is a map marker. Consult the legend: IMPRISONED. Entombed?

I'm beginning to become a connoisseur of my own sweat. I can taste the folds of not sweet on my buds. I haven't yet eaten from the body elsewhere, otherwise. Tired. The diagram and description is boring. I'll tell you why: I've done it a thousand times.

A tragedy:

A boy is born in the ides of March. His father dotes, his mother finds him ill. No siblings; one born, none mention-ed among the family. A day past the birth event comes the naming: Nice Name.

Nice Name is snipped then cries but stares, all under the close watch of the father, a grandly man, and his withering wife, miserly life.

The day comes for Nice Name to be taken home.

Greedy nurses prepare him. Father packs the mother things in mommy bags. He is near the door, glasses dripping off while he waits. She is frail, you see! I see alright, now let's go. Our son is waiting.

That's it.

I can't consult some internal ish. Bumps get stuck and loopy, not referenced, nor rooted, simply stuck. To sit with any burp for as long as I have sat with some is to lose. Nothing sounds familiar. In a field there rises; if I could only name it.

Children's Hour. I feel I should fill in some philosophy, or a more formal advice; channels can be changed. Here to. Let it be known that a man in a box is yet a man. A man buried is as lonely as he will ever be, and ever was. Walls move if you do not watch them. Never take the pill. Highly regimented diets of air will sustain us. Troughs are to be watered and pigged upon. Mountains climbed are no less immortal. The back of the hand is a ravine that should not be crossed. Never touch. The unremarkable sound that faints in your bedroom at night is glass shattering. Swallow when spoken to. Spit when exhumed. A tar-stained rope will never do. A year's worth of salt will build upon dank newspapers left quiet—ignore the patterns in the smeared print—they only forebode. Askewed and stern, default. Let the noises crowd each other; like tea leaves. And turn to the stars. Diviners are to be held in faith. The most graceful motion is a slice. The most noble motion is a feint.

Routine is a worse lock. Or fort of fate, a habit of bliss.

I can't keep up like this. Heaven is sickly, it's yellow, it's a stretch and covered in the chrome of film. Figure a layer. Meat.

I abandon so many bodies.

Here lie my habits: Biting or clenching, shoulder rolls, clearing throat, tap, the slip of tabs of poison into my rotwater or tea; stare into; chucking into the sink. That's it. See? The water is false. Just for show. What would I be then? What would I be thewn?

I used to count between the blooming of the hand. Never more than error, never less than X. A king puppet at the balcony. Questions remain, would surface like the bubbles in a swamp. Again: Dread in forecast. When once there was They, the day, looking back in bad health. Must payoff the threes. Keeping time was penance, and I am without penchant for that.

Smooth.

When wistful, I see myself as ember.

Transmission Stop.

Transmission Stop.

Transmission Stop. Stop. Cease semination.

Here lies the body of X-in-time, a man or brain that bears no remembrance. None of us gathered here may call to mind X-in-time, for he was a solitary (hah!) man, one that held congregation within himself. His soul, seriously now, no longer a part of an earthly body, may go freely into Heaven. XXX now presides in the body of—

A man roaming free on the plains. Cowboy of a man. Boy features. Manly, hard drive and discipline. Untaken. Not to be played, yet quivering. Breeding sensitive. Containing that multiple strength in multiples of ten and the frailty of a dandelion in a sour, shower, south wind. A lone drifter. Catamite. Drifting the plains, as he sees fit. Stopping for no man. Dropping for one. Bending, again, to no other one or will than his own, him, and even then, he puts up a hell of a fight. He's a man. Child! A high tale in wild—

Hand. Here.

Me: Convulsion box. Me: A dribble creak.

In fairness, I play dead; it used to strike me, render me dud and closed, its blown out phantom white seemed to access me, seethe on a mechanical plane; mold me reverent, as I had been found in that unordered place that exists only in trips. Fanciful fear. Then I fled. Now I stare.

I shall bite.

I know the hand, the shape and light of it, better than I know or ever knew an isolate of me. It, the hand, the light of it, is large. Thick. An attempt. Petals of puking and gulching light, of color, stretching, all orbed and swallowed in an invisible air of bubble list. A mean of cones or rays. Nor quaking. Held and hollow, up or right and in. Very soft. Let behind by gray crinkling, wired light and sound; all sound. Very soft. Gorged and iron, hot iron bent into itself, a ball. A swallowed lair. It's here. Or there ahead. I'm away from it. Familiar, I can breathe with it now—

Wait—

Wait.

In it.
What is it—

In it—no—
In it. Something. A square.

No—

In it. There, in the burp or fold or endless length and lilt—
It is holding something.

Inside, with the chimes.

Get them out—

Here, get them out of here. They are closing! They are closing, close please.

Please—

Go. Get it. What is it? (please) (god) What is it—

God could I move?

Should I move to—

Wait.

A square. Remember—remember the training from when you were growing, lucid scheming: Look at the thing then close your eyes then look at the thing. It can only be once. It's here—

My god.

A square, folded... paper.

Paper. A note.

That hand. (a note?)

What—

I can't reach inside it.

Were would it lead? What? Would it feed? Is it hot? No? My arm and hand, or—

It can't be inside—it is inside. Or not. (thank you) I have to. Would I be lead at all? Grabbed? Took? But what of the wall where it comes from? Where is—

You are not going anywhere.

So take it. Go. Move. Match it.
Can I?
My god it's full of—
Keep blinking (can never tell)—
The note. Only paper. Take it, coward, coach yourself and make it. Go into it—what else do you have left to melt?
Reach.

Closer. It is still tingling. It is still curling in waves. It's gray no it's white no—

Never white—

GET IT—

Ahh—

The black. Got it!

Blinking?

It's paper (here)—
Oh god how it feels (feel it)—
It's creased. Smooth it—DON'T put it to the ground
to smooth it, my god. The grime. It must be clean to be
read—
Read—
Wait?

Uhh—

This must not be! Rid! Can't be serious. No. No no.
Bring back the light. Swallow the rind. Where's the use?
It's here, or if it is it is maleficent. This isn't a shit! Not
eating or pissing or shitting! This isn't it. No. None or
nunc. Tract of not. Void. A void. Avoid—see? To be
taken. Granted, in the body, put. For me and me alone.
(but I built thrill here) Transmission stop. No eating.
Transmission stop. Transmission stop. Ahh—

Father's face, light behind him. An evening light. Poplar trees, poplar not because I knew them but because I was told: Poplar. Taken in his hands, gripped by my armpits, pain that would eventually spread through the ribs. His face falling, the sun meeting its gait and rising, raising somehow to become level. A yard, square, colors as they should be. Grass and brown rainwet gate, sun the palest orange, a prism on the royal glass. Smiling. Beseeched. Grass, all below me. I knew that it was then distinctly a game, the want to wiggle out of his arms and go feet first into his face. Little boots to teeth. And how the hands seemed to grip much harder, right away—

Stop stop stop, you've done it all wrong. It should've taken longer to reach in and grab the paper, right? You must manage yourself, fit it to form! No! See? All ruined. And where do we go now? Where do I go now?

If I had blood—

Dogs. Dogless home. Clean. Carpets, verses of it. Mom often on her knees to scrub the brown out. She teethed. And the cherry, the sulted smoke, feet above her, angled, reclined, aware in periphery. Labor believed. Hard labor. We must work our way into the world.

Why make myself in history now when I can do so later?

And I can work you out of it.

The homebody. The woman in bed, me at the foot of it. Staring. Her feet rising and staid as buildings. The covers a sea. The XXXXXXX a king. The large orange tupperware bowl upped with vomit.

Enough of this.

What of a fly for company. A fat one. Buzzing a blessing. It could feed on my shit. The convenience! Alright, alright. A plan: Make gums bleed, all of us. Drip. Intone the request on the paper. Slip it back; palm it, then move forward. Two steps back, snap. Step: Fly! Here! Fat as ever. Loud, certainly a spirit, or a child in a pool with his shirt on. Maybe merely a chain? Its links turn maggot. Never ending. A replicant behest: MORE REPLICANTS. And that is all. The protein of stunted pointing. Fucking. Chain ganging.

Our spiritual is sung alone, long, and echoes cordially.

Oh how a manacle would have changed things. They cry on the other side; the static, daddy! The static! And all is fixed with the tweak of an antennae. Coming in clearly, darling. Love, layers, swept.

Nope.

An investigative route would prove familiar. The paths

I've cut across this box are grooved, not physically, but essentially. Not essentially, but remembered so warped. Highways. Supraphysical highways. I've drove them, man. Come on with it—people talking in another room.

Joke.

Sleuthing. Corner to corner. Crawling on my knees—busted or bent?—and sniffing, a truffle pig in captivity. The utility closet: Shit and piss. The cobweb furnishings. The rec room: Shit and piss, come. One corner left, on the left—right—floor, leastly, for sleep. Ah! Cobwebs promote spiders. Spiders toil as genesis. So I've been backtracked and double-ceased already: The spiders don't exist!

Goodly, the concerns of the imprisoned are neither cultural nor transient.

Spiders.

Return to form. Breathing again, sitting while my legs are numb, and holding a holding paper. Holding. A paper. It is small and palmed. We are together now; a union I recognize. As one part and another of each other, the paper, its trees, and me, mine, my eyes. We are linked!

Chainless, but linked. We share in a slave song that inhabits our bones not for our benefit but for proof of concept. How about the mouth? Laid upon.

Heavy knuckles.

Hmm?

Chin down, peering over, brown rim of his glasses or hands. On the desk. Somewhere. Mine, maybe.
In a room.

Heavy hands.

Invisible ink. A hat brimmed with hairless hair, only dirty and seen when washed. An all or nothing proposition, surely; I put the paper down and rub it around and the grime leaches, the hand comes, and the paper stays black, remains, a bodily brine; or: A message. Revealed! And then placed back on the tray? Back with the hand? Or no! With me? Benevolently or indifferently looked upon; looked upon at all; oh let the poor boy use the light off of love to see the little message, cough, I mean, it's arbitrary after all—entertainment! Or: Let ye who hold no faith look upon Him, and find that He is good? Ringing from something lickable, the world will never know. We could, though! So, too, for, us, is, a, man, made, in, tomb—tomorrow.

Now there's a word that has lost its meaning.

And now for a little night music: Bread as water, water as feast. Feast as fodder, fodder as east. Yolk in brain and brain at least, udder for harp and bother a ceased—inhale! —under as farther and father as X, ill is scorn and tilling is fed. Four a quiver and numb anew, to ruin the ruins of razed make two. HALT—coming to a stop: Jury a witness. Sheep a wolf. When they cry FIRE! you see—

Cotton.

Memory, like a roadway, is emptied by plague.

Maybe I should have inked first, had my skin tainted. Tinted. Designs—de-signs. Marking and disfiguring, transforming skin, at least the upper dermis. Permanent to-do lists (get out) (don't get in in the first place)—dreamed misnomers laid upon. I could've at least imagined them, run my hands over myself and imagined them there, black outstanding. Perhaps I could've left a key.

Waiting is the name of the name of the name of the game. Third strata myth. Somewhere someone somehow counts black stones and white stones, placing them in lines. Evolving a hermetically sealed lot, free of lost causes and human wounds. Stones. Stones in a line. What is simpler? Safer? Cleaner? (why?)

I will paint a picture of my father the first if you agree to lock yourself set into this transmission. Transimmion. Bipedal blues. Okay? Okay:

Royal, or XXXXXX, liked to punch the air in front of our faces until the patterings of pressure made us cry as hard as the hardest did. XXXX, second eldest, knew the effect and purpose. Bloom, with a voice as significant as the largest tree or oldest stone, would: And that's why it's best to attack a thing in its infancy. Polio was a beauty.

Hah!

Your promise means nothing to me. I cannot hear it. Resume.

How about a culinary guide to paper? A canon for alphabites? First leaching.

The third moon is the soon moon. Gravity is grave, a flux. Unshaken. Not to be XXXXXXXXXX—

How better to bring you into, bring you in here? This is my concern, after all. I want you breathing in my breathing. Smiles. And smells! A tepid response. Well, you're only listening: At once and all at once it is awful. Was awful. Whichever hairs sensed ahead the dank boxly summit are now fried. I am a cleansed machine. In, and out. On my count: In.

And—

Out.

My low activity keeps the musk down.

I could tell you about the see-things, caused by prolonged exposure to dark, by prolonged starvation of light; light can be eaten. I've starved. A part of me was eating all the light of now and then in secret moving me. I have reached a plateau, and am middling, because the swamp phantasies have dried up. The hand, when it appears, makes all torrid. But, prior to its folding, in my wet period: Small hands emerging from hands, birthed and sprouting from all our fingertips, men with half a mouth enormous and full of teeth in retro, money floating and combusting in sharp tones, tar rain, the floor wet then upside down, my feet phosphorescent, my toes wrenched, oddly spaced claps at the highest resonance, ear quaking, everything in sequence, cancerous wire balls and mesh, bottles on the walls, the roof, wobbling back and forth in super speed, a man above light and smiling, the cell heaving out its carried by a double procession, elderly beggars marching toward something furnaced, black char, porridge spotted with white eyes and maggot eggs, white pouring from my ears, rainbows. Exotic locales and dance numbers. Slave extras. Nods, the feel of them. Here were some of the safer that I can recall. The rest will be away, please.

Some talking will always melt its forebears.

What, then, of a pen?

Overlarge mantises could be inspecting me. I imagine them matronly. Their arms folded, their heads swathed and their chests smocked. Green machines, full of mirrors. Medusas in clouds. Knowing, in vitro. Preaching telepathically but untouched by my silence: CONTAINMENT IS NOTHING—ALL IS CONTAINED—WHAT IS NOT CONTAINED IS NOT—trailing off as we override again.

You see? The sacrifices I make for—

Again, shall I reground? Should I bit myself, teeth the steel? Wishes and demands. Transient. I can slow an ocean only once. (no)

It's the experience of all young men.

...

Is it not?

A com—promise. Promise: I stop reflecting merit, you start listening.

Corn fields inhabited by the smallest men. Hunter hawks, starved and goaded into flight. The men curtailed, population monitored. Small bands of survivors thrive and pulse under moonlight, navigating by tactically quenched flame. The hawks moan in the morning. They rattle and dive with less and less frequency. The survivor bands learn the shadows and water and rare rocks. The monitors, backing their hawks, read the scouting reports and see victory. They move on. The hawks follow. At night, a safe month later, the smallest men emerge. They stalk the rows between the stalks in a timeless state. Left alone, they cry. They cry and touch each other. They see their mothers.

See the space between the corn.

I have something to say at an angle. I also have rare jewels. Buried somewhere.

A catalogue of catamarans for sailing types. Arranged alphabetically—

Closest to me now is my father. The closest yeoman. He held his estate and his rights as he held me; none could breathe.

Patter myth. To tell a lie nobly. Creation story. Birth parable. Earth mother, matriarch. Murderous father. Fetal brother. Golden touch. Sweetly sung, sinking boats, washing men ashore. One eyed things of strength. Lore. Fable. Ghost stories. Blood. All intoned in blood and delivered to another, passed as calmly as food.

If shot through a bully prism, we glean from the lean of the light this tale: Abraham. Closest man: Father. I could substitute but would do so without accurate aim. Closest man, a yeoman as well. Well enough. Fine and—

On the mountain. His son before him, back bare and pale beneath a fluorescent sun. Bending. In prayer. His legs clothed in rough fibrous pants, potato sacks. Shoeless. Hair cut as short as a mothered knife allows. Told now to pray upon the mountain, immediately, questioning the immed-iacy only once. Then stepping from his horse and handing the reigns to his father and finding a clean stretch of dirt to kneel upon. To bow. Now performing. And his father, rushed, eyes bleeding sunned tears and holding it. The knife less a blade by the second, the second regularly quiet, god allowing. A rage that stirred him into bleating vomit, to the mount. A returning cry. Questioned only once by his son. Blamed on the sun. As all proffers, true to the air of it. And now with the tool, held up between his hands, not in them, him weeping, but without speech, a last mourned wash to bestow to the lord a formed heart, one worth salve. In response a mountain as calm as it could be in the threshold without miracle. Royal, without crown. And a. And. And—

Knife down.

I need babied.

Mourning in days in which in ways in which I would not mourn, should not, as I could not mourn to full. The days and nights of old, day of stimulation. Stimulation breeding obligation, obligation in places as in things. The days and nights in which my heart would flutter and my brain would hum, I could feel it hum, I could feel it hummm almost as if the blood in circulate was charged negatively, positively—absolutely. Interior and anterior poll shifts. Locating the helix within you; earing. As much fun as digging up old parts, old bodies, dripped in black, a two-dimensional rainbow sheen. Ahh, a sigh: The old days. My patent days. Days spent and days saved. Solitude in public.

To the best of my ability: Dark. And within it, the
First Difficulty. (here) This is present firstly and promin-
ently: What surfaces first in sense? The smell of the cell?
The dark? No, not the dark, as the dark seems to be a
Difficulty that is prior to all other Difficulties and not a
sense or sensible at all; the dark is as much a genesis as to
become a pregenesis; that thing that is all want, the thing
that belies, that belies any order; god. Dark is, as, god.
And I within it. Dismissed, and nexting. So then must I
move to sussing out the first earthly and tangible Difficulty. What comes first? Sight—what is seen in the dark,
presently, irregardless of histories of maladapted eyes—or
Sound—what is heard now, and what has always been
heard; sounds of my body and sounds of the chimes, our
light—or Smell—which is a muck, and the most comfort,
as it, the Smell, in its muck, is a fire that makes me move,
the earthly thing—or Taste—which is always dry yet
forms a palette—or Touch—which can be lost with a hard
enough telling out, as I am now, as you are witness—or
Else?

The First Difficulty.
Smell:
A stew. If the floor weren't so cool I'd simmer. The
square air seems to be a constant and unmoving humid
mass, ductless, unsucked, not at all hovering but an

invisible cloth or sauce. Goose down without the small explosions. Reduced down to bubble. When I move about, in fugues, or to keep the body primed, the heat increases. The humidity follows. What I am left in on those days is a box almost bereaving. Drowningtime hallucinations were familiar; I tried so desperately to swim up. And now, in my calmer state, in this broadest hour, the air seems to do its best to impress and let the cool off the floor work upwards, rise. Let it rise, I take to whispering. (let it rise) All of these details, the state of the air or what's left of it, add up to insulation. Smell, the pugnant, is quick to strike and mood in shifts. Like a swamp filled with battling viscosity: Oil slicks and crocodile shit and runoff. A now and newly almost entirely predictable cycle. Murk to muck to must to murk. My sedimentary deposits in each corner—the come, the shit, the piss, the spit, the skin—seem to float and intermingle like partygoers swollen with liquor, frequently vomiting on each other. Rarely do I take in a sweetness; the smell is always a hue of sour, anymore. Maybe it once was sweet. Or never.

The Second Difficulty: Sight.

Was blind, tied upon, as if a black handkerchief rested on my face, firstly tied and then pulled tight and tied again, little, stripping me of sidewalks and peach trees and dogs of all breeds. Public, depublicked. Vanishing. Motor functions waned like mooned seas. As my balance went my head lolled. Two concussions counted, many others felt as I stumbled about this space in search of growing boundaries; stumbling, only to find that the walls were as fixed as my plane of sight. Lost amid a growing set of paths and autonomous squares. Fixed and lost. A deepened gone. Something I could count on. It was with this, the realization of a present fixture, a certain lack, that fed me and kept me gaining; feeling and using my fingers as eyes. The parts are elastic, capable of rebounding. I was only shaped as I myself wanted to be shaped, I would say, sometimes out loud. Shaped. An orb among geomes. Corners and intersects, running lines. In despair I would blank, and then come alive thinking of the walls. The floor and ceiling an exclusion as if I could escape only through running—physical channels. Not fly or dive, dig, climb. Walking or running, toward a horizon. I must return. The Second: Sight. Sight. I eat sight. Another obstacle: Monsters. Poisoned teeth and cave throats. Eyes that bright; the light was what scared me. Again, must I derail? Let me—I will—say. The lacked sleep, the sleep that someone else claims for me—beach front? snowed in?— sometimes gathers and finds me and knocks me, prize fought. Ashamed as I'm knocked back and away from clear transmission. Channels muddied. Not that I can swim, anyway. Also: A perpetual and acute awareness of throb-bing. A throbbing born in the back of my head and stemming out in waves to my nose, collecting with it my eyes and forehead and skull and sinuses. All pushed forward, called to attend. Sharply saluting. I'm sure that if I could see, or if baffled in light, the throbbing would go. Blinking becomes aristocratic. Con—comfortable in saying that, in dreams, my eyes are still.

The game in which my mother slept, my brother fainted, my father climbed the stairs. Rules unique. Setup approximately three to four years. Completion time forty five minutes, dependent upon discretionary habits exercised in bathrooms with visual aid. Operatives and agents. Cowboys and indians. The yeller and the snuffed.

Placed on a spinwheel and spun. The fingers above you sticky with meat. Cleaned only after a second turn. Cards drawn. Professions picked. Paths. Incomes. Squares determine your fate, and a wheel, but the squares much more; the squares defined and always shifting color but never really different. How little I knew, then. How I should have washed the meat off my fingers before—
Paused. Bricks broken, chasms jumped. Danger narrowly avoided. Royal boomed: I hate those fucking things. You want to control something? I'll show you. Little heart hopes for a missing mother, a day vacated to a mall or worse. Ceilings and low walls pale green. The sea haunts, even without eyes, the sea haunts. To return to smell: Salt. Salt is a prospect, a nurse, a favored customer. Salt always comes back. Tail wagging. Solid. Safe from boots.

Most arguments: This isn't what it should be. The better arguments: This isn't what it never is. Nothing touches—

I'm kept company. You see: The hand. It's a friend. I'm sure you—

I'm sure you—

But does the hand ever leave?

The timing! Quick: Huddled, the hand must see me as such. Huddled in the corner and sniveling. Although: No. Again. (no) Not scared. Insofar. Torpid. Diprot. A palm-less cypriot. How this affects the Difficulties? How it asserts them. Don't be silly. Don't be stupid. Don't be indulgent; no pretense. Hand. Check. Light. Check.

Pen: Check.

Pen.

Paper. And now: Pen.
Pen: PEN. There.

Engendered. A danger to ourselves, right?

A fucking pen.
A fucking. Certainly.

Another invitation to grab at it? To grab again? I should shout an inquiry: AM I A DOG? DO YOU KNOW I'M IN HERE?

A pen would be too convenient a symbol.

Do you realize where I am? Do I?

Benign, the hand has been, and patient. The white pill was passed on. A supplement. A get well soon card. A truck. A boulder. The square that I've thumbed and all but eaten could very well contain my passage out. A map. A key in folding. The pen a supplement. A thorascope. A weapon. Or: Toys. All is toy, amusement. Closed circuit television and me a star. Memorabilia with my naked form: Episode 100101001: XXXXX pisses in box! Shits in his box! Sleeps! Legions from the highest regions. Hordes. Trolls in underbaths. Approaches teem with posterity, admiration as ploy. Or perhaps the hand enacts a session of monument, a procession, building, pill (none) to paper to pen to a baby sun: a baby sun, spinning on a gentle axis.

But, ahh, with the pen I can test this room for slope like never before. I would grab the pen, lay it down, watch —no, listen—for a roll. After all, common inertia was stripped and laid bare long ago. Forced to adjust. I could very well be living on an inverse plane. At the very least angled. Much rarer. Finally I'm given a measure! Blessing! Blessing!

Could I draw the shape of this? Could I mark the shape of blank?

Paid: The days of logical lubrication. Looks in books. Tracking. As I see it, knowing is a feature for those above ground. Abandon hope. Invoke your right to wealth.

Invitations. The pill: to EAT. The paper: to CRUSH, to EAT. The pen: to FEEL for INK. The pen: to STAB.

To stab.

There, a light; revolt. What about that? What would He say if I attacked? Royal. What would he decree? Praise, surely. Praise and then appraise. Must be scored, everything must be scored. Bowel movements, quantity and quality, stickiness of lingerie catalogue pages, bowls of blank eaten, mouths fed, sets of wheels, geography. A constant syllabus, a constant index. A private consult, though, and not open to the public. He, frail near the end of him but always kingly in spittle and dip, belonged to the family. Belongs ever still.

Inhabits. In, habits.

So what if I did pick up a pen and bring it down in the hand, set it into the mold of bright, given without fear of a swift retreat, me nearing. Can it smell? The white white— so near yellow—contains something in the thread of it, it must be power. Or what if the hand, upon nearing, screens full of holes and puckering blood? And then: What of my company? In what proximity? Blood is not vapor; blood is a human trail. Are they there, one to each side of me? And what of above and below? Why don't I hear them, their moans? Movement? The thought of it all nearly stops me dead now, on the far wall. The horror of others supersedes other horrors. I'll take the fucking pen, then. I'll move it. (see) But first, moving forward.

Now, as the feet move: A little provocation, some needling. When the pen is taken, what then? Is there, in my hand and heart, a vocation suddenly formed? Responsibilities and regularity etched permanent in residual dust. Herein lie a father. Hush. Hurting. A transmission, no? A set, a string of code, manifest and deluged. And after all—an audience? The old story of fallen trees, their sounds; a potboiler, the end-all question of that century, science pegged a footlength behind the capacity of design; that of: In what motor lie the I? And is it shared? So, for one like me who cries in public—but let the ions and tears merely flow positive; the contemptible is best coveted!—let me scream a bit and claw at the rafters while being torn toward the floor: A boy possessed of toys is a boy until someone speaks.

Another plod up and another string: Seems to me cells are to be escaped. Cells. We leave both and we are free to roam in lattices of light.

A pen! We cordially invite you to—

THE NUREMBERG TRIALS.

8pm. Look sharp, be sharp.

Step, repeat to come. What of the unseen thicket? Its disappearance? Mourned are the days in which sailors and colonial postees are torn apart by phantom creatures— ecologically fondled then left to dry; possibly extinct—in savannas, mourned are the nights in which knees are cut on bristle. Retreats seemed unlikely, then.

No.

Another step, halving as I go. Avoiding, clearly. Feigning mistake. I must take note of permutations of the piano, and my god how they've warped.

Nearing.

A slow dread found alone in old media. All of it: It's all a filth, but not junk.

Now—

Here.

It is, in cylinder. How a meaning, an arrived essence of a thing, when fixed, memorized, made rote, how meaning circumvents the stuff that gives it reference. How reverence is removed. How the thing continues, as itself, above no beyond—no outside of the thing. Words reached around, the light, its patterns, grasped behind. A sonorous fucking and dragging away.

Oh how the quality of mental health has declined.

White palms again.

With my back to its light I am a cast and a mold. Aware of this. Also aware of how not I want to move. So I won't. Better, yes? The pen (nope) in second order sight. That's how I treat free misgivings—
Turkey, and an elbow emerging from a formerly gobbling ass. The emerald glass, hilted, slipping down his nose over and over, the free hand to push them back and come down with forefinger and thumb and swipe away the grease on a nose. Hard job, this stuffing, he decreed. Hard job, he decried.

More of the illumination roulette. Let's say the hand

sees true and witnesses my back, the pen created and taken. Might a reward be waiting in light? As long as I stay fixed, a gloss of white cherish. Ehh. Can't chance it. Must remain mobile. The forgotten paper. Couldn't bear to see the glyphs on it, if they are apparent. Ready to ship.

Closed. Roulette spun. Ball on black.

Here I am again with my tools. How convenient. What comes next? A cave fire? Perhaps an oblong stone? Bone piles? Fuck. Toss it.

And now I cannot ever let the paper drop. Blank! Palms up in surrender. Wares the white pill, waves the white flag.

Body in degenerate. Feeling for mirrors and nothing more. Sifting for a solution; my hands will sweat. The grime will coat the paper in time. But: Who says your hands are clean?

Smile, ladies and gentlemen. Smiles.

Computational species. Full of circuits. Not brimmed with grey zones, free of flush quarters, throbbing and lay flat, pings of the highest frequency. Or everyone's at lunch.

Lightbulb! Click. Solution forthcoming, must warm hands—

...

The solution is in folding! Let me explain—autodidacts flee. The tiny slip of paper seen here can very easily transcend its spatial bounds! For, if rightly folded, the paper, like magic, ascends into a central position in its containing room and floats there, as if hovered by helium fog. But, I assure you, helium fog the magic is not! No. For a limited time only, order today and you'll receive a second copy of Float The Paper Indefinitely for half the price, that's right Half The Price. And what an easy solution! Cue: Chunk Mom. "You know, I just—once I saw it—just had to have this solution. You've seen it—it's incredible! And the folds are so easy and take very little dimensional time and space. You could do it covered, is what I'm saying. Completely covered. I'm wary!" Act now and use your second copy as further proof that the first copy was sufficient! Yes! You could lose it all! The Float will outlast you! Call today!

Either that or I try to find a soft spot on me, free of excretion. Then, using that spot as a sort of landing pad, keep the paper on weight for entirety. Laying lengthwise could prove viable. The dimple in my chest.

Brick by brick I have to sweat. Motives. Light benign no more.

Possible.

How many engagement rings have I swore to you?

Hungertight.

Have you noticed the propensity for grandiloquence that marks those locked away? Performance is the key. My bible is full of negative capabilities.

Shocked. Shocked that I've passed over a startling potential of the pen: To wound myself! Kill, even. Wow. The pen, the point of it, could also at the very least become a jam for you. For us. The code string could halt and bunch up and then dissolve, for I could strike myself with aphasia with half the force of a levered fall. I see the speech regions. I have faith in my abilities.

Perhaps those outside—dare I glance away from Outside? abandon the term? their is always a container, prerequisite—expect me to feed on the lot: Pill, Paper, Pen. Three, five, three. If a peach pit comes next, slimed and brown and shrunk in that bloom, I will suspect numerological foul play. Patterns were promised away. Struck through with a—

We'll take that right out for you.

All of it?

Look at what I'm doing.

Swipe. Swipe.

My bible burns of culpability. It sings like the thrushes.

Might be encouraged to sketch. To map, plot, assign some depth. Detail the shit in the corner. Render a clean page, the lack of flies. Dot vertices with precision. Sculpt the air.

Agnosticism as foreplay. Coy little girls.

Or the pond in the northwest acre, the tank. The barbwire line run across it. The first time alone, crossing a pasture full of bramble and cactus and arriving near dark and seeing the long black snake twined in the barbwire, perched and looping. Dreams of fires diminished.

Sutures clipped off and served as candy.

Man-height towers, individual, spotted grey and lining the horizon. Castle keeps. A maiden in each. Small black windows empty of broadcast. The maidens kept off, in power saver mode.

Hmm. Mmm.

A compulsive man in an institution. Committed. He wanders the halls, per regular history and suggestion. He rubs his hands together. Sometimes the skin sloughs off. Often his fingertips are dark as cut beets. Prowling. A gentle one, though, the nurses say. They pass one another, casting shy glances his way, as if he's the only one with any dignity. Like an animal in the snow. Haloed. The man spends his days walking, and in the evening he is fed his pills and food with care. Spoiled, the other captives think.

Spoiled one. Baby. In between their howling they come to the windows and watch him pass in the hall, unsupervised, frequent and floating. Time passes in crosswise brown shadows. A clock settles—orderlies descend, the monkeys howl, the man is bound and carried away, struggling, put out. Rough. Hands lay him on a silver table and strap him down. Leather still warm from the grip. The men over him blocking a small light. The orderlies pause, then pass out of the room. Moments. Left to himself. He touches the cold metal, his hands, his ass, his back, but his hands matter the most, they feel cold the most, more importantly they feel bare. He wants them covered. He cries for it, he cowers. The rounds quicken. Breaths catch infrequently as he sops back into his skull. His fingers unmoving as the rest of him shakes. Unmoving. And from the innards of the ward the monkeys cry—

Are you surprised I haven't peopled this room? I have, though. Look: Anna (hi) and Charles (hi) and Catherine (hi) and David and Christopher; their eyes are opening.

It is unbearable to imagine those pale and groveling, the lot on the streets. They couldn't even eat after seeing their own skin-stripped forms; their horrible moss of veins.

Chew. Oh my god. Rancid rancid rancid. Keep going. Down to meal.

The Third Difficulty: Taste. Nights we would stare down at plates forbade. Kept clean until the simmering crockpot was dropped among, we were left to dig in with our hands and risk the grime underneath our fingernails shaking loose and dropping into the boiled, or our skin pickling and blistering white in tubs. A soft scrub will do, from downstairs, up from his chair. Gulping and hoping for a near miss of footstep. Leave the stairs, daddy. Leave the stairs. This coming from the little XXXXXXX. His hands were small and mealy. He puffed into rooms. Or the shaken soda treatments. The meals out were few and tense, the lot of us mannered but all at unsafe distances. The tables were always circles, and I wondered even then if the strange hosts were in on something. But better to use utensils. You're kept scrappy for a reason, the red carpet moaned. Don't get use to this. So we would swallow and little ourselves, hoping to go powder, and sink into the tablecloths. In the evenings we could lay down alright. Quartered with due respect. Left to ourselves until dawn. Belied of chores. Snoring. I made sure to stay awake past XXXXXXX and make sure that nothing erupted. It was in those nights I took to the spinning nausea. How I couldn't close my eyes without feeling amid sea. Land-locked yet surrounded on all sides by valved and rolling waves. It took years to figure or find a salve; I had to bunch the blooming gag into a black mist. Let it all twirl, let my stomach disconnect from my spun head. Separate entity. Gather up what I could and not focus on the motion; constant falls from the bed, as royal had set it high on blocks. But the mist, seeing, helped. Helped me but didn't save the little one. If there was a common ancestor among us it was saved in the boiling pots laid out before her. Before the high-on-high descended.

Before a swallow let me hold it in my mouth, let it bleed while I list a list of appeasements to myself, provocations to the hand and those outside: Here is what you've given, here is what you've taken away: Contractors and their bloodwork. Humane societies. Border patrol. Spark plugs and topiaries. Budding young breathers in open relationships. Automatons. Glossy paper. Stock. Employee penchants. Underdogs. Overseers. The sweat on fluorescent light and cupped condiments, stacked. What to eat and improper burials. Ritualized sex, mass murder. Hysteria and strikethroughs. Parking lots and pantheons, gag orders. Rotten honey. Champagne flutes and communion. Careful consideration. Suspect prostitutes on middling avenues. Housewives. Guilds. Anorexia nervosa and stop-loss. Mea culpa.

Gulp.

Ahh and the hand again. So soon? Oh, my metric audience, need I re-render this flirting? Cast it newly, amid different light? Take me to task. Critical analysis, although appreciated, will have to exist as a cast-out phantom, for interpretive morale—or: Not sensory—cannot travel upstream. Blame the broadcast. Sorry.

Anyway: Here a hand. The Hand! I must formalize. Why didn't I? Perhaps the paper taste. Campfire sentimentality. A breach. Back clear. My motivations doubled? To eat or not to eat? What to do when the blood is real?

The Hunger Diet.

The No No No Diet Diet.

Now. Now I must concede:

God.

Uhh.

God is empty and only big when first.

Clean.

Laugh track.

Ah hah! Oh the drama! Look at him fuming! His cheeks read red! His lips a purple! His ears a convex current of steam! Let's hold him down and fill him with opiates.

Comedic timing is the password and the puppet string of mind.

If you've been accepting admission for long you can probably see the patterns, right? I oscillate. Frequency determined by some scapegoat. A nailed goat, crossed up and bleeding from the hooves. From the pierce in his ribs pours fur and faith.

So what to do in my vacation home? How to put my starter wife to work? Where are the kids? Where are the kids? Is the crack in the foundation moving? Are the cupboards on a slant? Is the milk sour? Is the car crying from the brake pedal? Are the bicycles rolling flat? Is the sky ever red?

I've swallowed my Jonah. I've swallowed my reed.

To take large communion in temple of the sun, nearing phosphate. To hold in. To pore blood. To spin mission and all inside.

Yes I've taken the home into my body yes. Yes the body cannot beseech me yes. Yes the home is buffered from my breaches yes. Yes the rain cannot enter yes. Yes the home will not tremble yes. Yes the body is a shelter yes. Yes the home is an earth yes. Yes the home is an earth yes.

Beetles, mewling, crushed into paste. Scrawled to make the scarab text. Torches curl ash against set-stone walls. Incant. Incant.

You have been indicted by all history. Your charges read thus: Preach when you can. Lie down on the hour. Place the hay near the potato skins. Be red. Feel the sun. Harness the creature with hair for eyes. Bring in water from the slope. Discard all periphery. Maintain arthritis. Contain the privileged, use their bribes against them. Place your feet beside her when she sleeps. Lower yourself.

I used to tap out war games on the wall. To remain close. Fake an amateur knowledge of other codes. Arc my fingers for the trace fire. Call in support.

Immortalism is never dead.

God I've got it in my belly. Hymn for me.

Mmmmmmm.

Another mockup: Be directionless. Lose up, down, left and right. Lose center. You find that time goes with it. Progress slowed to an amber, slowed to a sap. I felt crystalline for months.

Precinct nirvana. Rods wrapped in scripture, meant to

strike.

So indulgent to list those who proclaim death as the cycle makers. Better to list those never born. Subsist on ceremony. Rely on ritual.

Grain theory. Committees of contracted farmers. Grain silos, a tower. They are meeting places. They are gathered around. They seem to always host blue skies behind them. One is framed in wire and rigged to explode. The farmers watch at distance, behind a clear barrier. The charge is set and clicked, and the plains roll a seethe wind. No go. The farmers stare ahead at the still tower. They know better than to look away from a miracle. As their eyes water from the glint of a sun held rapt, a perfect column of grain goes skyward—

Done with deja vus. No, my slice of plane isn't running into others anymore. It lost stasis miles back. System malfunction. Flashes on a brightboard.

Roadmap: I swallowed the paper given to me. I swallowed it in pieces. Mashed, it still lives in my teeth, I'm sure. So to, for now, how to now and for.

Young men carrying folded flags. Toddlers carrying cardboard cutouts of dead mothers. A parade of swarming locusts, trotting badgers.

Fill a room with folksong and combust it.

Have I departed indefinitely into seas of phantasia? Should I consult a rubric? I'm not in a rolling phonebook, but between its pages when flipped. Do you see me now? Where the ants line. What the grass, maligned, bends toward. I'm in your ear and your X, the shadow of the line of the muscle of your back. Also: Empty cans. Rolls disposed. Bread balls. Underneath the riptide, the water that never motions out to sea, never motions in to land. The channel. The channel.

God how I hope I fixed that faulty wiring.

If I see your mother—

The wall! The walls! I haven't thrown myself against them in so long. Oh, what a shame. Let me, let me, shall we? Oh honey shall we?

Blood.

Expulsion—corners. But blood—in the center.

Your face is only a map if it can be recharted, no?

Cursed so quickly, I must heal. Another fuckaround.

Do you plan to accept the XXXX XXXX XXXXXX?

...

Many, many terms. How I wish I could forget them all.
Barring forget, lest let me feel them all again in a torrent.

Pardon the interruption.

Shall I—knees—bring you up to speed? Put you—palms—on the level? The—foot—up and up—foot? (up and up?)

Trivial, but once again I have lost the wall that opens. I suppose it's cardinal. I suppose a reminder will come soon. I suppose I've lost it. I suppose—

Hmm.

And why is the ascetic so noble? Why not the many manned lover? No: The obsessive and the rigid. Formality a mere contempt. Do we, wistful, wish after them for their little violences? Their neglects? Do we admire them because they self-cut and self-cauterize? Do we admire them because they adjust in their tunneled travel to accommodate? Do we give them benefit? Why do we admire a machine so marveled and contemptible? Why do we long for a present object always receding?

Genius is a holistic therapy.

For those of you who drone, let me apologize for not going murderous. A: I shan't be in the middle of a plot. (earth alone) B: I shan't be shading. Nor do I cool, nor do I turn. I am forever goo.

Necrotic? No: Even then comes a breathing.

Have you ever smelt a foundry? I, for one, think the smelting belongs only inside the castings and casings, in the molta that fawns and spews. Shy away from the gloved men. Shy away from their sneers. They are all teeth and pallid glint. They are all down and receding.

Okay. I'll do it. I'll pad the melodramamine. But now you realize you're unfortunately hooked. Once before, I promised I'd never promise, no? And without a fortune to spare we dive:

The stomach! O the stomach. How shall I lock what's inside? Bear to be the truth in me. Bear to see the proof in thee. Bear to knee the thief in me. Bear to be the me you see. I'm losing—

COULD WE—I—postpone the bodily business— SHITTING! PISSING!—to another—relegate it? Could we—I! I!—take myself into a low mode of coma dome, manufacture a steady somnolent state? NO, NO—what about a total tear of all that's known? HAH! HAH—or a plug? WHAT?—a plug! A PLUG—yes, a plug. I could keep myself plugged! I could back and back and back and —STOPPAGE? YES! Now we're—I! I! I!—getting, now we get it!

Boiling down the billed words; take atoms in sludges, thick against the back of the throat and as bitter as any mercury, here or not. Truly—membrane as my witness—complex. Little reactors, we are. Bumbling along, nudging each other in lane changes as the space splits infinite inside us. Remember: Mimesis is our great grandaddy, our big mother. Lest our copy painters cry dumbly, let us sing them genetic praises! Let us share our genetic expressions! Let's fuck.

Coyly I return to plugging myself. Should I? Dour days, folks. Dour days.

All-night telethons on grain-fed televisions. Speaking in reverse. The blue condolences. Soft touch withdrawals from a hemmed neckline. Under tray, on mute. A mountainous terrain, aural, phonic—escalating screeching. Cash appeals in front of us matched with the staving sort behind. A familial and familiar sideways nod. Brother eye lock. Pulled into the ween box. Behind us a range, behind us a teleplay.

Burn the senate with no one in it.

A sweeping orator:
CAN WE NOT AFFORD THE DEAD A SIMPLE

GRACE? A SIMPLE REGARD, WITHOUT SENTIMENTALITY OR STATURE? ONLY AFTER WE ARE LEFT WITH THEIR LIQUID MAY WE THANK THE WORMED FOR THEIR FOUND-ATION AND SILENCE?

Totem counting. The whole tribe run together and crowded, flinching, investigated.

I'd bring up the rare musical loops if I hadn't brought up the rare musical loops.

Does the hand want me to use myself as a spigot? Does the hand admire thirst? Is thirst ever seen?

Once, I found fears of gas chambers.

Knees like knuckles, patterned with bite marks. Tooth mosaics.
Repeat.

How do you feel?

...

And now I don't describe the paper because I can't.

Under beaded whip or metal flak, hand drawn, I would probably profess to cyclicality. Under local anesthesia, I cry light.

Can one be axiomed without jury? Without trial? What about hung and supposed? Superimposed? Plotted?

You see, I leave the questions when I weave. When the thread comes together the hand disappears. Godly, I know. But even this is among itself, and trapped, so help me sing.

Ain't a performance without a frame. Ain't a shoe without a sole.

And in the valley there were kings. And in the valley there were kings who rode. And in the valley there were kings who rode pale horses. And in the valley there were kings who rode pale horses into flame. And in the valley there were kings who rode pale horses into flame beside red lakes. And in the valley there were kings who rode pale horses into flame beside red lakes, mountains weeping. And in the valley the kings knew of metal and knew of stone and had dominion. And in the valley the kings laughed. And in the valley the stones sang. And in the valley the kings awoke in stupor. And in the valley the kings were visiting fairies. And in the valley the kings knew themselves. And in the valley the kings were made of rock and made of steel, and kept the fairies to themselves, and fired the lakes from all sides, and wept horses, and buried mountains, and felt themselves alone and red underneath a great weight that is always becoming.

And since a pill can throw a body into The Great Fathom, The Place In Which All Resides, Nirvana, A Temple Among Innumerable Leaves, I say Fuck The Pill and Let Us Rot Inside Ourselves, Be Trapped, Because Without A Call There Is No Road And No Reward, and For That I Am Grateful.

And I already relayed my comedy.

What then is left in the digital guide? Who can you find in boxes? What's to buy? Where's to go? Do palm trees sprout in nation states? Do the refugees build in prayer? Do mud leaves lie unordered, left in stacks, not being thatched into roofs? And who counts everything? Where are the records kept? Will the ink dissolve? Will the ink—

Member the motor took.

I can't keep carrying these things; stigmata. The little lapping ocean—topcube, roof to another—below, though, promises to dry whatever rain has been bestowed; make the paper dirty and smudge the pen. Well, god, I'm just stuck.

Sniffling. Hugging myself.

Must strike out all the softness. Record: Rely on me. Kemp me bare.

Wait. Phantom draft. Surely mistaken. A notion of wind is... null. But what it brings me to? Yes. Hand. Yes.

How quickly I forget.

The paper chase. The paper chase! It's already in my gut, goddamnit. Churning there. Outlasting its host I'm sure, winning champion medals and crafting an electric current, like a big wheel stuck in saltwater. And I could chase it with a sword. A metal rod. Conducive—conducive!—to my audience, I'm sure. Another antennae, this one lockable by X-ray and electromagnet. A beacon to industry I'd become. A hero, a champion of fidelity and technology; a truly modern man and thoroughly oiled filly.

Bear with me. Bless my internal logic. Bless it now for it's all that sinks. Our anchor. In time of storm it is our anchor.

Vitriol from the mother mast always promoted bitter sleep, but sleep. From the fearhead, wavetaker, we were hit. From the mother mast we were hidden in orange satin and left to daylight. Doorway maritime battles. Skirmishes without hit, sink. Water left running after the mascara seeped down into the pipes, ran away from the fevered fingers, ran away from the howling mouth. Take a hand into your hand, bring with you a flashlight. Make shadows. Make faces.

I feel the fingers of wonder. They are pregnant and laced with indescribable color.

Laughing! Laughing.

To focus on teeth: Oh you know sometimes I wish my teeth would grow in. All the way. Fuse in the middle and become a plate of teeth. Tall enough to always force a bare, a smile.

Talk of plates: The ones below us. You assumed—us an abandoned term, an abandoned stretch of grammar. So: Me! Talk of plates: The ones below me. Talk of plates: The ones below. Talk of plates: The ones. Talk of plates: The one. The one plate. All one plate, with fissure. Heat.

Remember the days of profession? Of both kinds. One in the same, really. Does the sickle form a soul? If so, only in crescent moons.

Remember the days of temperance? When the minute hands didn't melt down into stripped, clean-on-the-edges sludge. When the tale had a tail. How the mouths were soft, then. But were they ever soft, son? Are they ever hard, daddy?

And then to humble oaths: The roar, jet screams. Lawns left off at half past street, fading completely by the commercial zone. How, from above, the earth looked like a strobing. Finally. An inarguable pattern.

And how, like in a combustion engine, the spaces between explosive motion—when captured—all caught the same frequency and idyll light. That was the secret. That was the entire secret of an entire age.

Let us rest.

Will I hear crickets?

Two feet through the door and she's saying where is the haircut? Where is the haircut? Where is the haircut? Where is the haircut?

I have a slipshod temperament; a proper dementia. If you want clean lines, learn to ice skate. Here is mud. And if you finger it enough and if the rain is becoming hard enough you can probably find, in your greaseline palms, the further: I cannot promise a codex. I cannot promise that from now on there will be a return to framing. Said: I cannot promise that I can continue to speak. I cannot

promise my lips to you, dear. I could tear them off for you?
I could create such wonderful bouquets for you, darling. If
I had just the, just the right angled flowers, the marvels. I'd
promise you, a promise, they would pour forth from my
hands, dearest, they would pour until you could take it no
more, until your eyes could not contain all the light I
packed in vases.

A lull. Ahh, without the hand in sight I'm given too
much. Branding libertines in dreamtime. Torture porn?
On all walls, blazing and daily monitors. A larger cube and
a larger cube, nest eggs, surrounding and surrounding and
all enveloped in each other with nearly enough space in
between for separate and circulating atmospheres, each a
box, like this box, growing more and more full of higher
and higher transgression. Placating. The matter at (hah!)
hand.

Can you feel the contours I'm setting out for us? There
is a large basin that we must dry out and seep into and lie
within. See?

How lowly! To neglect the matters at hand, namely:
Thing. Paper. How can one even begin to speak for
oneself without an intimate knowledge of the miserly

suffering of oh! Others! Weeping fantods. Exhausted mewling. There is but one answer for those of us lucky enough not to scrounge for food or fend off rapists with engendered arms: Speak! Speak from the thresholds of all the Others! Speak with their heart in your throat, arteries pupping blood from your lips in parallel to a sad, such a sad and beautiful song. Let me begin now! Why all the nervous circling? Ahh! Let! Me! Are you watching? Eyes. Yes. Begin! THE PEN. How roughly I'm handled. The nobility I can scrape together from piecemeal moments, rememberings of myself in promised times, golden golden golden, keep me alight and illumined and trekking, always trekking forth into a brave and exponentially brutal reality, a reality filled with STARK conditions, but, here, watch, because I'm allowed to MOVE YOU! Here I am TRIUMPHANT! INSPIRING! My capacity to do something! Ahh! Look here because I can write! See the ink? BRAVE! And I'm held until I snap shut again. Okay: Bravo! Moving on. Address the players. THE PAPER: Blank I am. So lost and blank. And fragile. Easily ripped. But then after a long term of handling I'm kind of set down softly with some newly pressed paper around me and suddenly I'm not so lonely, but still crying. A CELEBRATION OF THE HUMAN SPIRIT! Okay, and then some more. THE SHIT IN THE CORNER: I stink. CUM IN THE OTHER CORNER: I'm spent—a diminished return. THE SKIN FLAKES: Musical number! THE SLEEPING SPOT: Obtuse but likable. THE AUD-

When Jesus cries there's far bleating.

So hip these days, to be of wavering number. A one man zoo. They pry at the bars, I bare my teeth and retreat. This push pull forms a sort of suction that attracts the local birds. Swallows dive inconsiderately. Popcorn is thrown; they block the view! And oh, well, I can't really be presumptuous enough to believe I can refute piety without getting pious. Another trap. Thank you, non-atom. Thank you, pictures, windowless facts. I'm feeling sprent through campuses. Total—in one sense—gateway drug.

You've jeered I think. I can smell you. So: Stand, scuff back. A pardoning. I'm going to lose the you.

See how long I can do that?

I fear my eventual transcription. How will the space be assigned? Will there be space? How else can you fill a blank? None of that stuff; light's in high demand.

Bulb breaks in his hand and a seep of crimson fleurs. Motions blend from that place on.

The wall with no doors is of no concern. I hope this is as certain for—

Only flesh.

You must people the void. You must? How could you leave it? How could you? There's motion implied! All around. It has to be in the space. This is no deep space terrain—wait—this is no unimaginable fold—wait—this is no—stop here. This is no.

It begins as a small bother, a miniscule bloodline back of the earlobe. Brush at it. It returns, brush at it. It feels negligible. The rest is smooth and not attended. After an inordinate amount of calming, reached a strait in which body became an absence piece by piece. Now an earlobe calling. Brush at it. The lack in between noted, made sure, brush at it, not a constant presence, this back earlobe. Brush at it. Bloodline. Faint. Note the procession. A calming, due and promoted and practiced, brush at it, until an absence achieved. Brush at it. Have to let the vein fall away. Have brush at it, to let the vein fall away. Brush at it. The back of the earlobe. The head. Brush at it. Pulsing. On the fingers. Note the fingers, clean brush at it. An angle. The legs underneath you, absent. Move them, note the ankles brush at it and the bloodline. Ankles rush, crush. Brush at it push it away. Ankles hot and hitting, brush at it, scraped. Blood underneath. Hands are clean. Note the hands. Note the brush at it, wall. Note the wall. Breathe, feint, let a bloodline. Note the. Breath. Brush at it. Ankles. Shift. Extend legs. Flatten, then. Brush at it. Note above you. Blood. The smells catching up. The bloodline. Brush at it. The smells coming up. Ankles torn, torn and note the note the, fresh to air, straighten up. Inordinate calm brush at it. Inordinate calm. Brush at it. Breathe. Straighten up. Brush at it. Feint bloodline. Note the fingers, clean. Clean. The blood back of your calves. Stay and promote calm. Brush at it. Feint let up. Catching up. Smells, back of your calves with blood. Brush at it. Ankles and spread up the bones, catching up, bloodlet, the breathing brush at it, calm. Inordinate calm.

The total force of all people suppressing terrible acts is the total weight of god.

Screed passed through the noblemen, fellows in ale, dropped to the floor at night. It corralled attention. Said: Do the opposite. Set eyes in paranoid lines. We look back on ourselves, the entire royal court with angled faces.

There, eyes aligned; a plane, a grid.

Yet again the pen. How can I play father when song must be lost?

And the much blanker, the golden loom: Paper. Is it paper? Or is it skin?

And I thought a door would show after the consummation of X and shit. After the consumption of shit, X.

No plan to render time into a ledger. No point by pointillism. Instead: A tuning fork.

Like putting down dogs for economic reasons.

Now it's time for candy code. Communicable waste! Keep scouring, though: The attack plan, Laura Lee, comes when you're dozed and cast in half-light. The concussions come in sync. Swimmingly. The city burns.

Counter intelligence reeks of sex.

Knowing my toenails, it's easy to play the politico. The dissident. And how you'd see me faint at the pulpit.
Counting veins.
Huge razing wheels tear through it. Sunspokes catch in the foliage, even though—
That man who once said before where there was word there was mud, and I told him: Before there was mud there were poisoned wells.

Give me your labor.

A singing exchange. Fair trade.

The man, cellared, with his stack of myth. He dug for years and never found bottom. Stars are named after him.

By now I've surely dropped it. (by now he's surely dropped it)

Remember: I can never know I'm staring.

There is a general mess of twitch muscles, and sometimes they freeze, in cataract, and fire all at once and guide me into a hard surface. Set reeling, they'll go again. And again. Little pools will drag at my feet and spread. Slick is slick no more.

The Fourth Difficulty: Hearing. Little boys in nursery rhymes: Nearing. Cut to: Frothing. Cut to: Fearing. Guards, near space of hearing space: Leering. To themselves: Jeering. An abandoned game: Cicero. The ears caught in a perverse relationship, that of touch and go. I still celebrate their movements. The tattoos, such. A high trill. A low and wavering vibrato, filling the gilded lilies and maids, the men already forty feet down the street, out from the opera, hats left behind in every other seat, house empty except for the hats, and the maids and mistresses are all in brutal rupture and nearing a drained death, one inflicted by the vibrato, the total face of the missus a howl, and the slow glide from the doors to the stage, above the gone heads and the rocking hats, each empty seat of red felt quivering by the fine hairs, moving, tandem to the low no, moving down, toward the stage, the vibrato does not increase, the vibrato nears but does not increase, and you:

Perhaps you should thank me now.

If I can recurse enough—loop enough then I can stall it. Remind me of my mechanics. Ehh—

How long ago I decided that broadcast is binary. Lamentable. If only I could've spoken in gels.

There is a better notion of evolution. It takes polar night and sets it stiff in its shoulder with—
Measure. The hands weighed. The hand waits.

I promised in blood that I would not embody the weather. I gave it no voice. How the ribs call. They re-angle. Positioned for a new metric of waves.

No difference between the trenchant and battened dictator, my body: We both, if we could, would flatten it all.

Apocalypse lost meaning when boxed.

What?

Treacherous bonds of diaspora. Wait: Do not transcribe the signal with that. The signal is good. I am not ready to be dispersed. Still new. The prisms are not nearly vast enough. They would reign, and the body would cede mountains. Capacity would suddenly become cancerous.

Prone.

Prone. Locked in, paper and pen! I would jaunt in place but the grime would slip me.

Where is the hand? Where is The Hand? That is what it is. The Nursing Mouth. The Slitted Shin.

There is something behind me.

Prayers come in like a service. One reads them, One dispenses with them. They are made into a paste and immolated. One and One hold countenance as prayers come in. They are often made of whisper, but the ones saved are made of salt. There was once a prayer made of an entire city. There was once one made of a snail. These were held away.

You can let me have my singularity.

You have filled my hands.

I had this until—

You can keep me from bending. Is that what you are?
Are you a molten blind? Do you straighten when cool? Do
you mean that faith is had, that there is an opportunity not
for resistance but for acquiescence and that you must
come, by establishing my hands as strung up, come into
this room, now that you have held me, can you also make
me talk in turns, can you also make me lose my eyes, can
you also put shine on my cheeks, or here I am moved and
you are to blame. You are to blame. Not taken by take but
taken by gift. I'm left with two devices, both for experi-
menting. One is a unique system of gels and drying. One is
archival. One is only One when there is a void surrounding. You have collapsed the support. You. The walls
were once meant for an air, dispersal, for a negative bind.
You have given me with a picture. I must color. You have
given me raw eyes and raw color. I am keeping within an
in. I want an in way. No out way. An obvious inclusion of
out way. The stroll of light past a bare arm. The mooded
culp of a soft reach. The horns. The machine pre-talk. The
eventless night. I was granted haven. I was promised in an
office. I was ordered, not shelved. Left closed. Seamless,
seamless only as a notification that symbols too were cooed

away. A notice. And now. This. Tools. I will only wait for you. I could only recognize a pattern and appreciate repetition. Found faith in recursion. As expressed. Then promised. Then, now, given away. A small shift to you. A small shift. Might, maybe. You have betrayed artifice. You have shown a cheek with no veins. No. And now the palms filled with skin again. A motive. To embody. Quaint, I'd say. Yes, quaint. Such a debt paid to the past, liquified. When in that short history you've acknowledged something former and living. Foolish. But not a fool to knave and know. A fool shown. Certainly a fool shown. How present. What an explicit gesture. How laden with invitation. Could you not have been less so? Could you not have been? How you've given in to, hmmm. A shame really. Could you not have given in to you? How naive to think that all is not plastic! There are many viewers, many providers. I am still in grace as long as you prepare. I haven't lost my becoming. I have never, never lost.

Come back.

Come back to me, baby.

Feed me when I'm mewling.

Take down your estimate.

Here we go.

I feel it.

Grate change.

Grate change.

No change. No speaking. No speaking in the living
room. Keep that shit to yourself. Keep that shit to yourself.
A draft of palm leaf. Get the FUCK—
No. No, now I am sure of the intercepted and decoded
rays. How else to know not to come? Listening! It's
listening. They are realizing: Take me and wait and do the
opposite. Do the opposite, let me in.

Cut my support. I am unstable and rotten. I am a debt. Toxic. I am spilled, a hazard. A premature extinction. A death toll. Subprime. I am ill-handled. I am a fee.

There was unbuttoning, and his chest. Nothing more.

I need to make you feel better.

how? how how how how how?

A diamond.

It began in a river. Boys and girls played in the water at dusk, when the mothers were cooking and mashing together beans and germs. One little boy, a bright little boy, and handsome, was ankled by the river which was now just as much a stream. He was looking at himself in the water. He was looking at his eyes. He was looking at his hair. He was thinking about his mother and her mouth saying You are Handsome. He was thinking about the moon because he felt it over his shoulder. The children around him didn't pay much attention. Handsome Boy was also Quiet Boy. Handsome Boy was quiet for no reason. This is what they, the other mothers, whispered about him. They were jealous of his good looks. He was bright and and the best looking, but he had no father. For that the other mothers felt fine. And Handsome Boy looked at the water every evening. Sometimes into the night. Sometimes he looked so far into the water that he could see another moon, a brother moon. He knew that it would be dumb to reach down and try to scoop it out of the water, with his hands, but he had tried. Only once. Handsome Boy was now ankled in the stream, looking at the water and smelling the mush. The other children made no noise. They had stopped splashing. Handsome Boy was broken from his look with the water, by this no noise of the children. He looked away. He saw their faces. Their arms, little like his, wrapped around each other. Their knees, hobbly like his, bent. Like that. Handsome Boy saw their eyes. He followed them. They led back to the stream where he was ankled. He saw up the stream and into the stream and saw a diamond. A diamond. Like the mothers had talked about, that stone they knew all about. Handsome Boy watched it come down the stream. It was big and it floated. It looked like perfect and it went back and forth like wine. Handsome Boy could see the water on the diamond and could think of the diamond, and the boys and girls held each other and thought of the diamond, though some wouldn't know. Handsome Boy felt it stumble in the water, but soft, as it came closer. But some wouldn't know. Handsome Boy put his fingertips in his mouth and knew that the boys and girls who weren't in the river and who didn't know would be the ones to go to their mothers and be better, back when the moons were out of the water and the diamond, a diamond, had gone. Handsome Boy let the diamond walk by. With little feet in the water that kept it up, because it stumbled. And Quiet Boy kept his fingertips near his lips. His eyes had followed, and the diamond, and the water, and the moon.

Stealing is transcendent and more bound to cosmology than you'll ever know, and I also do it.

A break in me. The lung games. Often forgotten. Played only by neophytes. Hung up in the shredded rooms when done. Foreign and dominated. Pleasure, while players sense inertia and all come at once. Coach: An intercom, but live and run with winks.

Zone is an understanding. Void is a brother. Space is a lack of sleep. Learning is a function of never leaving. Never is a relation to mirror. Zone is a callback to relations, their relations, and that love is a picture of ice. Understand? Understand? Correct? A rainbow is only tempic.

I'll leave you to intuit. Obviously. What I've given you is a plate of inedible fruit. You can leave it rot or watch it or eat it. You can eat it, though. What I've given you is a plate of inedible fruit. See?

Watching me.

THE HAND IS HERE!

    No. Not honest. I see the contract. Yes: There it is. My XXXXX is written on it in an ink I don't recognize. Take the ink off. Take the ink off.
    Pleasure pleasure pleasure pleasure—
    I've got to get some principle again.

The longest you've endured, my dear? Please: Hold out your hand. My god, what a fine glove. You, surely, know the finest things.

Allow me to walk you through it—oh, watch the stairs, watch the stairs. They're deeper than expected. And the heels—I don't know how you do it. Please. Right this way.

Ahhhh—and here is the central landing. Yes that piece was brought in by my grandmother—a patron late in life, all sorts of fine sculptors. Yes, that one is quite famous, actually. We've had people from all over come to see it—I just watch from the windows. The help charges admission. Ahh! I kid. I kid I kid—come. Here, watch the cobble-stones. That grass has crept up around the edges in such a peculiar fashion, don't you think? Hmm. And here, this magnificent—oh, please do—yes isn't that quite a full sound? These magnificent doors are late exteenth century. From a Spanish oak. Taken from a stripped monastery in

BEEP. Oh, why yes—they were neutral. And like all neutral things, (breath) the world must... touch every bit of it. Was what, darling? What was what? Let's continue on—this is the main ballroom—

Cut the shit.

Count the king.

Bury the horses. Do you see the labor? My back is basically breaking.

Did you know that phantasms first appeared in wax?

You are formally contained to the territory for its entirety. The ball begins and ends at midnight. The theme of the evening is 100,000,000 Pardons.

If known, a place is a known plane of planes in space unknown in their relation to the relation of the planes of place. This is in my blood.

I admit: The stream is there. Remember?

Or take a plane ride, set yourself there. Feel the layers of full air on each side. You must imagine first. Measure. Then, know that a name exists for the full air on each side of the plane in which you are laid, and that the name is only discoverable through abandonment. But then there is a layer of, a bevel of, useless space, no plane at all but a static, sorted, in between. See it and now you cannot see it. Hear it and know your ears would burst. Feel it and know your mouth would swell and cry. Sense—know the planes around you now are the planes in which you lie. you have left the center again—

I can't help but laugh.

A national poll: The morning brings everyone awake, and wears them formal. They are cast to each other on freeways and broadways. They are made to eat food. Lights click on in intervals. A national poll: The sun at night or moon in the morning. Are the rays meant to be castrated. Are the animals to be kept on provision with gag order. Do the stones set in a row, do they, should they be moved. Is the speaking voice still proper. Was the control collar a viable—thing? thing? was the—control collar? And then: Boom. Hands sweep aside the ballots. A nationwide sigh as magic goes away. An internally circulated grin at the success of a self-effacing, disintegrated voice. COSTS become an echo in tertiary space, and as it passes the satellites and diode cables, the astronaut feels it move up through his feet and out his helmet.

Lapse.

Numbness in the shaman. Cry for that now.

Or if the wall opens and offers a child: I will beat it to my chest in the just-dead way. I will sob for all mothers. Sob for all mothers, like good myth. Obliquity in worship.

Tertiary space. How light might come in.

I have run a gamut of plague, or akin of plague. First: Little hives. Then swollen tongue. Dry eyes. Unconquerable thirst. All this in rapture, obviously. Then: More thirst, mighty as before. Then boils. Blisters. Tongue unswelled and reswelled. My throat felt the tongue go and went up with it: Swelled shut. Fingers bent when I couldn't see them. All the time I couldn't—can't see them. My lips shook. Ears oscillated, spun around on each side of my head. Like plates, and that was awful because putting your ears to the floor only revealed the—

I have to reconcile these things, don't I?
Should I put me on to the other? Should I talk?
My faith is in you, dear creatures. Please please.

Should I mark?

Like a plummet to the sun, it's all so gone.
My color prohibits much going.
I can plan, though.
I can plan.

Or better to stab myself. Stabbing myself, I guess.

Although: What if I remind myself that eternity is simply thinking?

I can only while standing and only while warm. Edicts in a mother tongue out of a father. Pleas. Whimpering belongs to the dog.
And sheltered!
A just, grass square. Border patrol set up and off-dutied. Sleepwatches. Lit from and under some orange. How cavernous we felt. Like wind.

The magnolias—

Better at spacing myself out, saving myself up. Rounding up the pennies. I can't slip out with wet fins if I'm jarred and stowed. Like the old ones. So I emerge in vinegar and wait awhile. I can announce myself and return fresh. There will be a center, held by a massive rally, during still night. Quiet and freshwater eyes will lift themselves up, pan up, to the night sky, and heaven will not only be waiting, heaven will—

Or fucking myself in the corner.

Scraping the skin off.

Like the newly red ring around it and all the gagging. The smell in the trunk after three months of that blanket stewing.

See?

Here, Step into my—

Two losses make big wins. Big returns. You just have to move back and forth between them.

Ahhhhh.

You see it now?

I'm ratcheting.

And I feel your eyes.

You're clicking. Back and forth.

Big returns.

See the film?

Pardon the interlude. Watch—

There's a difficulty of stomach, somewhere. I could address it. A churning, simple enough. Wherein the insides eat and ate each other. Wherein the lining began to fade and stuff spilled in. Wasn't much to do for him. Ease his pain, like war. No self-needling, though; we administered. The boy suffered. We did all we could, lest he save himself with the alternative treatment, which was a nightmare in itself.

Me: For the sake of this interview, could you provide details?

(sigh) Well, I suppose. Starts uhh, with a hose. Thick. And that hose is industrial strength, and works under all sorts of high pressure. The boy would've had to take the hose into him. Understand? And let the hose feed a sort of paste—a starch. Loaded with tracers. And the magnets come and pull at the color and there's your, there's the monitor lit up and you can get a map, where it's going. But after the hose you have to seal him shut—

I couldn't resist!

With the slightest pressure I can confine a path of destruction to a pinpoint. Smart bombs.

I always say my genetic disposition. I always say my geographical disposition. I always say my sexual disposition. I always say my faithful disposition. I always say my political disposition. I always say my disposition.

One of these is not like the others.

There is a lineup, stark faces. Eyes like rough sewn denim. Devoid of glint. A ma'am behind glass. A mister beside her. In between them, the glass and the lineup, there passes a judgement in which one is deemed to stay forever, or a multiple of forever or for some time, in a space, which is determined, designed and built by another one with the ability to uphold and record one's history of upholding written on paper, and the one past glass, judged, is the one who lives inside a space made by another who is taught how to design spaces like this. It stops here.

Oh! Hah!

Are you comfortable?

Time-lapse and a sleep switch: Invest in those technologies.

Also, space is not painted.

I may have mentioned this before, but its hard to track your own dog days.

Death, though—

Dirth—I'm wandering. If the sun hit my back I'd go forever. Dirth—I go casual only from your ears. Dirth—if you listened somewhere else, or with fever, I wouldn't—dirth—is it time again for royalty? Dirth—royalty seems to run, lately. Dirth—dead ends. Dirth—like X. Dirth—seven bits of something and then you're dirth—here it is—one too many.

Chocolate cake or slice of pear? Chocolate cake or slice of pear?

A distillation, fermenting myself: Trust me! Trust me I would cry for it! For you and only you. To get you trustful and appreciative of each other!

Fuck that latter part. Poison breeds poison for a

reason. Seasons pass.

I have gone on too long about light.

Men and women lie in ice water. Their animals weep at home. Their electronics flitter out. Their grass dies. Their trees split. Their water browns. Their numbers switch.

Pen and paper.

Or if I speak too directly, you'll know the ruse and refuse it—you'll shut off. But but but you can't because how direct can I be while I'm still coding? I'm not dual channel. You're dual channel! I'm piping this all the time. If you see it in layers: If you see it in cake—
There is a mistake in the frame. There is a mistake in the painting. The mistake in the frame and the mistake in the painting inform each other.

Neither can sell.

Or bribes.

The legal process: Necroprosthesis. Assigning new limbs onto old bodies.

A picture of the cave is in every dentist's office. You can find them.

Or an indirect route to malaise—a middle year woman, pale sculpts and plains of cheek, high irises. In the kitchen, in between bouts of cold tap, the noise catches up to her in a television way, and it's not distress but a call, beneath everything, the real layer exists, it's just behind enough of it everywhere, and if you start to tear away all around and in the walls then you will find it.

Not alive, though.

More in water. Falling inside large bodies and smaller rivulets. Feet slip and shoulders overtake—

Perhaps I should eat shit?

You tell me. (can't resist)

If this box is spinning or circling with me in it, then that fucking hand is the gravitational lynchpin. The box is being straitlined out, away from the other boxes. Or not. Presumedly—one can presume—there is enough space assigned to each cube's path to allow for massive stretches of shakeless carry. We all orbit. The hand though, the hand gathers at a center and spines into all the cubes like a fungus. A two dimensional hand, someone's sketch, exists, outlying all the cubes, their dance or flight or XXX, and is infinitely less capacitive, but is able yet to reach into each of our privacies and ruin them whole.

A holy order of salvage.

Acres of wholesale, waved away into a sluice dump.

Please do not assault me for answers.
To feign an answer is to play a dismemberment.

I do sing for hire. I'm a high tremor.

I've extended an invitation to dance more times than
breathing to you.

Take—

Can you bring anything with you?

No.

Can you leave anything behind?

Here?

Yes. For right here.

I can—

Light!
Light!
Color!
Light!
Light!
Light!
Light!
Light!
Light!
Light!
Light!
Light!
Light!
Light!
Did you get all these?
Light!
Light!
Light!
Light!
SOUND!
Light!
Color!
SOUND!
Light! Incrementally I'll do it—
Light!
Light!
Light!
SOUND!

LIGHT!
Color!
Light!
Light!
Sight!
Color!
Clolor!
Light!
None.

Now he focuses. Stands up, draws breath. Slowly exhales. He looks ahead but not quite. He keeps his eyes from straining. He reminds himself not to look out too far. He's stronger. He's wiser. This is his moment. This is his time to shine, his spotlight. His moment in the spotlight. This is his moment. He stands. He stands and is ready to deliver. He's stronger. He calms himself, collects his thoughts. Gathers his wits about him. Is stronger. He collects his wits, gathers himself. Cool, he exhales. He draws his breath, he stands. He stands straight. His back is stronger. He backs himself away. He draws breath. He's cooler. He draws himself up. He strongs himself. He gathers his wits. His time to shine back, spotlight. Time to shine spotlight. Time to gather his wits and back himself strongly, back to his spotlight in the back of it. Strongly. Gather his breath back and strongly back himself to the breadth of it. Breath it. Breathe it strongly and wit gather himself strong it cool it strongly making force of it. He's stronger. He is wiser. He is gathering himself, about to strongly. He is about to deliver—

Aria.

Or, as a boy:

A sick wind rises up. It is unhealthy. It isn't cared for. It is a wind that has been left without other less frightening winds. A wind that has no way of its own length, and reach and height, above all. A wind, young, that derives its power from forward movement. Leaving behind all it can, including the knowing that it will, full well, come back in circular ways to where it began and was born, a wind without ease. Unease. A diseased wind. It knows it can only circle before a gradual disappearing or dissipating or placating sadness. And so the wind cries, not in song but in motion. The wind is crying when it runs through the cities that touch a certain height—cities with buildings large enough to call. And it cries when it knows there is an answer behind it. It moves. It always moves. The wind, though lonely and sick, can take itself around the world, or around itself, an equally as circuitous and impressed feat, in less time than it takes for the men the wind winds around to realize they've been left behind by something that moves forward much faster and much better than them. The wind is not pride. The wind is sick. There is not a cure for the wind, there isn't a cure. There is no diagnosis. The wind can only allocate itself to itself, can only cry because it knows the very motion it uses, forward, not back, back would only be forward when trapped like the wind is trapped, so the wind can only move its sadness into a furtherance of itself. The wind is immortal. The wind is cherished, though. By the men and women it warps around when the weather's right. By the calls above the buildings—they're known. By the ones who bear it. By the parts of itself it does not know but knows it does not know, by the same parts that do not know they do not know, they only know, like the wind, that movement. It is a forward wrapping circle. The wind cries. The circle does not change, as its only is forward. And the wind, who is born sad and cries to move, does not think about its height or furtherance. The wind sees the wind ahead of itself. The wind an impression of the next wraparound. The wind, because it was born a very long space ago, knows its lengths only in regard to the changes in face that the men and women make with it. The wind also knows that, as it must be bound by a stream of itself—a space unlike the wind because it is not a part of the wind, it is a part of itself, and a part of itself, and a part of itself again, until there are no parts but only the spaces between—the wind cannot move alongside itself like the men and women can. Because the men and women are all the same. Their faces. They move alongside one another and have that union or that left behind sadness that the wind cannot fantasize about or dream about but knows is there. Feels in itself, but only in motion. Another—not another, as the wind cannot know another, or two, or one more piece—please, the wind must run by its own strength of forward motion. It can move. It will move. The wind is a will. It does not know this, as it must be still to know, but it does feel. The wind feels this. This is the secret of the crying and the sadness and the diseased circuit—the wind does a sensing.

It senses without itself knowing, like numb parts of the men who run alongside each other, or the women who smile when wrapped around. The faces do not know each other, but the wind senses. But the wind also, while moving, feels in it that if it stopped, the sense of itself, the wind knowing that in its motion it is a motive and sensing thing—it knows it can stop. To stop and be still is to not be wind but space. Filled or not. Air. Wind, though born, feels unknown to death. Feels itself to be known only in moving, sometimes achieving the same place in two circles, sometimes wrapping around the same faces—all the same—sometimes in fear of its birth or fear of its sadness or fear of its ceaseless motive motion or fear of its sensing, knowing, fear of its not being wind. Fear. The wind is fear. The wind is fear in knowing. And the people who run alongside each other can only block their eyes, shiver.

You want a history?

I am shouting for XXXXX but an empty room is coming up in place. Maybe that's it.

I move only through hunger. Find some parallels while I eat the stuff on the floor.
No, that too is an attitude.

This is medicinal! And it's working, honey!

Come to and imagine: Massive piercing light behind a hard smile. That is infinity. (I invite you)

Like lace interiors.

There are three keys. You may have them all by now. I go no further.

There are two common objects. Demystify:

Right hand left hand a more formal mode of electrocution or soliloquy an ancient device framed by throngs of goats gathered to drink dark milk from a mother of the sybil child king who cannot sleep and instead blurts little bloods out his eyes and bleats like his pantheon of followers all a grand theatre piece meant to rave the constituents back together after the long winter shepherd's war pike use and falconry or science jump cuts to three thousand advanced metronomic gunplays and sex play and forgery of genetic switches a smell lingering a dumb pastime—

A dull pastime.

Like a bulb emulsed in kerosene, from which the bastard roots grow: The rhizomes grow heavy among each other. The roots sprout then curl into themselves. The roots behave under just law set out among the other bulbs set in kerosene. The roots have no fingers. The roots can breathe. The roots are quantic and contained. The roots have no metric. The roots live around the bulb but also independently: The roots are new material—the bulb emulsed in kerosene does not recognize its lineage.

Nor the wealthy patron who burned the city.

Or the liquid addict.

Bring to me an understanding! Are all good men gone away? Are all mothers old inside? Are all daughters tired? Are all animals pure? Are all rooms gates? Are all mazes hiding a deeper, lower maze?

When I was in a mother I noticed all the people could not stop reaching out, out out out, from themselves while not at all knowing what was two hundred miles beneath them.

The mouse's convulsions——

Complex instruments. Dirt. Story. Milk and matrices. And honey. Hungry.

Platitudes——

Or new fire.

Can we label that Black?

Surely.

Thanks.

What's——

It's of no importance.

A general thing.

Porcelain deposits.

I cannot say I'm tired.

Is this about the abandonment of a remedial logician? Fill me in. I'm sure of it: This is a brush and odes of paint, it's all black, don't worry about the holes, fill them.

Please decode me if you think this a cry in a century. Please unlock the walls if you think I'm a decade's concern.

Hurry to the wall! Hurry to the wall! Get above it— the sky's lighting up!

I cannot think of municipal fireworks. They inspire another song to lying. Their construction. The stench in which the ladies work. Belts. Acres of belts. A rolling space. A star eye. Wicker scars up and down his chest. His allergy to belts. Tomato juice, whirred and poured—a whole bath. The orange tiles—

Should I command myself by number?

Should I provide myself more space? Let me just call someone—

I once birthed a birdhouse. I found myself singing in it.

In between fits, again I am haunted by singing. Remember the opera? I cannot claim, or fill in, a body or voice. I can only show you the disembowelment beforehand. My stomach lie resting on pueblo tile. My knees drop and touch, but my head is filled in with a stark blue white split desert. I am half in and halved. Tenuously holding—

Back to what which cuts like crystal and belongs to the same humming.

I wait long enough and I can thrive all of it in code. You'll take years.

I already said fantasia.

Great anxiety about the machine. Used to be. To feel another moving thing; it had life! I felt I had breasts. I felt braided white.

In a proposed jewelbox: Math. History.

Have I told enough? Have I outweighed a persian thousand? I have markedly been less faithful—to myself, too many. But, in null: I have forgotten what was promised for the end of the scaraband telling, I have forgotten the cloture—

Abandon me like sand! Feel the ocean instead! The waters are romantics—the sand merely a plateau into a moving field. Love the water! Leave the sand! Leave the grains of days! Drown. See if I keep you buoyant.

Threats and lies and jests and prods and promises and coos and softs and lows and hysterical highs. Pornographic highs. Thoughts of such a when when one could send some to shivers. Childlike excavations and latent pig images.

Please, please please please—

By now ... By now he must've dropped them.

No boss he's stronger than we imagined—
Hah!

Tommy self-castrates. He makes the clippers go snap then wilts.

Fuzz, videotaping, laughs hysterically.

See? There's marginal use in bread and butter.

Can you both deliver a thing and withhold it? The live act projects its death. An overwhelming thing? Good too well? How do I make a place live and die? How do I return the animal to a lifeless living? I need to put more of a dent in god.

Hurry up, sit up, shut up, be quiet, quiet down, hurry, shut up, sit straight, shut it, hurry it up, shut up, sit still, shut up, hurry, quiet, shut it, hurry up and sit still, shut up and sit still, sit still and shut up, hurry it up, shut up, sit, shut it, sit still and shut—

Variety is also a way of decreasing.

Dream in a land where water knows its fluency.

Hung, a miserly wither. Barely wider than the pole. One piece of bread at his feet, the rest dropped on the dirt, many below the platform. A road nearby.

Is it now for gratitude? Is it now for stretching? I have no way of showing the time. Are you tracking? Keeping up?

I held my stomach to the right wall right in the center and waited. I held it there in the longest shifts, longer than real, and it or air never came. (can't be right anymore)

Sorry to be so vulgar, but: The ceiling is not low enough, just a bit high. And nothing I stack in the corners provides any stable height. Squishy. Nothing at all fits in this room! Smiling!

It was also a sport to fill this up with weather. (was) To imagine a boiling snow wider than first apparent, plumes and decks of it in draping, calming near my top inch when laying down, and finally whispering like all soft snow, and when it's so near, the space becomes unbearable: Latch! A pull to my skin, and then melt. Never cold to touch, though. Always warm.

Stars came, but the stars spaz out.

There were living room signs, all to deal with sadness. You can pick it up, he said. And that. And that, he said. Keep cleaning.

Mother blurs.

Nearly as vulgar to give you mother than to fix on piss and shit. Vulgarity isn't murder, it's arson.

Presently: Floating.

There's a record of aphasia somewhere. I've put in a formal request, but nobody seems to understand me.

By now my hip is bleeding. The scabs used to build, stack up. Like a temple. I could almost assign levels: Here is bestowed the colored crown, here is a view of the highlands. I could not disassociate the royalty.

Shall I trumpet? WHEN MAN IS LEFT TO NOTH-ING IS IT THEN HE TAKES AN EMPIRE?

Those mantis eyes.

Pleasurably.

How can I be both scarce and abundant?

You'd think by now a market couldn't encapsulate me,

finally, now, conditionally, it loves me unconditionally. Some market. A little storm churned up with cream and separation. It will go and curdle. Under the new moon. So temporary.

Pleated born-agains at the door. They seemed to be more welcome by the carpet, all brown. Only welcomed for a minute. Rabbits.

Echo level bullshit. Pond equations. Nearly mythical arcs and propositions on a shale slide, down to rock fort with the rattlesnake missing. The humid and the orange.

How prone I am to slipping. It's as if there is a funnel, sucking down toward a dark spot or shut-off place, with the looping water a deposit-filled slick of chlorine and my own baby sweat. You see? You just did it! You just did it, sweetie! It's okay!

Tactical infusions: Tempo and the boiled of threes.

I can blatantly embody just one being one—being myself right now, for now, and say: The whole word is a command. Noel.

I shall gather you here today to praise a man lost to us, a man patent with flies and full of shit in his mouth dripping shit out his eyes and ears and pumping shit from his guts out his shoes and the coffin spilling with shit and black flies coming from the mouth of the pallbearers and shit stewing below everyone's feet, all fleeing, a shit lake that deepens with each passing word of the preacher himself a passing word of shit falling into himself in a lake of shit and bubbling up from his eyes shit and the coffin sinking—

HOLD

Hold now

Hold, please.

Did you catch them? In the space there? Like fireflies.
Let's—

Holding patterns. Are best left. Off. Of.

Theres a family down there!

An anesthesia of purpose. They take you into a chair
—no, it's comfortable—and let you look at magazines and
wildlife until you slow. It's all administered. Yes, there is
steady supply of looks-over-the-shoulder. Negligence is
left at school. Now you're dead. And wise enough to take
that figuratively. And sleeping. And the sleep they place in
you so carefully is the most deliberate and wonderful sleep;
it's as if floating isn't an idea anymore. Then comes the
check. They firmly displace your clothing, rub once over
large sections of your arms, legs, chest—it's all very
routine. Once over with the gloves to make sure nothing
attaches and starts to go. No, no, not morbid if it saves...
Yes. So, once they've roughly gone—AND SAFELY—
gone over everything, the other three are brought in to
watch while the other two are dismissed. Break. The local
slowdown—mine, not theirs—takes awhile. Then the
three administer certain utilities. And the three—NO—
they come back, and take care of you once it's done.

You're done then. So calmly they bring you back to life. They let you look at yourself with the room full. Mmhmm. No... The time will come.

Debriefed in line. Taken into an office and led out, a simultaneous flow of new individuals needing to be briefed and debriefed. As they file, one notices a nick in the fabric of the right cuff of his white shirt. To check his watch, he sees the nick. To raise his arm to straighten his tie, he sees the nick. The nick is all he sees. As a steady flow, the line of yet debriefed lessens and lessens. One once said there is no pace in this place, the one that once told the him who led the her to a date, once both briefed. On the date the two discussed the nature of the brief, the information he had been given, uncut information, kempt, neat and under-standable like a wooden diving platform on a small lake. He led himself to her, then he led himself away. Not unlike the line, which now had dissipated to just one who had yet to walk through. He checked his watch and nick. She sig-naled him and they walked past one another, him on his small way to the door of debriefing and her on her small way to the door out of the holding hall that led to the debriefing room, the little office. They passed. He thought small thoughts and felt clean, but not like he had before. The nick suddenly felt enormous, cutting up his entire sleeve and peering above the lapel of his coat, just obvious enough to signal those who had the information, the debriefers, the information like a diving platform on a small lake, the ones both ready to debrief and ready to dispense with the notion that the information, the clean and kempt information, could never really be taken in and accepted and acted upon, because such information would never be so clean, they were there, and such information was a nick of information, a small cut near the edge of something much more vast and empty.

However long I trade with you is the time it will take to unpack the wares I receive. The expanse rains dust.

The two lovers—
No, not just yet.

There are these waving lights that must flash at you. They do, I can feel the light on your face. Do you feel them? Do you feel it? It must be warm. If it is warm and if you feel it, you have to be moving further. You have to be asking yourself: What bulb is behind these lights? And then: Is there a who behind the bulb? Is there an operative hand?

HAND.

Might a placenta slip through the door in the light of the hand?

By now, you might've guessed: I've abandoned all the paper, the pen. It's okay.

The vital words are now passed from an undercurrent. The belly. The infrapower.

A terrible amount of matrices. Within the legs, do they connect? Or are they more and more flattened versions of the lines before? Can you put them in a flow at all? Can you take them away enough to look at them on the outside? No, the answer is always no. The factoid is a no and a game of throat. You cannot exist in the sphere of spheres. You cannot thrust yourself outside the web that includes multi bodies, bodies everywhere, strung up and flies and open mouths.

Sunshine Hour! (interlude)

A self-referendum on sainthood: Me! Or: Is it proper for the saint to establish himself as saintly while breathing, taking in water? Is it possible? Let the electorate show that I deem myself worthy: But, in want of dual things at once, and in negligent acknowledgement of the the other, third, formally above-all notion of not-wanting, of zero, of hum, then—am I ineligible? Or is the saint known to himself as a heaven holder. Do they confide in snide terms about the light behind their backs and the men and women far below them? Joan mumbles, too. Matrimonial concerns: Do

saints have them? Marital strife: Not in a box, that's—
hunger? Always. Doomed? Not for long. Please, let me
cast myself at your feet and mourn my placeholder image:
That man standing up and looking down upon his tangible
form, as the man in hologram is the true body and deserves
a place in heaven. He is the saint: I am no saint. I am
rightly burning myself, only to dissolve and show you, in
my ash, the form of all of them behind me. General
rapture. Ash pokings. I'm at all the trials, though. I have
seats beside the first woman near the back. If no woman
rests: I am standing, four feet above the upmost man. I
wait like this, in lay, and count the penance stripes on my
back. To tie a whip around my feet. Or self-castrate and
pool in myself: To leave another form of me in white
around red. Self: Cast. The ballot boxes nearly always
open, as long as the maw of indexes is still seizing, as long
as our voice still sings and heals in nodes.

Divinity in copies.

Never a fair day, in waiting. A knuckle sized up. Held
aloft, near the eyes, in a guessing game from the brother
fare: How cubic? How round?

That's it. You've seen the heart.

Autonomous union. Marriages in bounds. The most
solvent in all imaginable ways: The officiate, the bonds-
men. Massive, surflexed influx of capital. Prenatal leanings

like: liberal, mathematical, rearing. The simple wit of
dumb questions a sport and a hobby, but only feigned in
public. Ferried away in carts were the texts of odious
origin, the smelling salts. Pleasure was relegated to domes.
Answers were given in obsessional, torrential waves. Not a
seeking, anymore, but a drowning.

Know me? Saying? Palms, fist, up to eyelids, and:
AHHH.

Like the rare occasion when the eyelids try to rise on
their own: That lifting? An uprising? Never an event
because of the ties to the lower lid, ties to the back lid, ties
to the skull. A checklist of pheromones. Yes: Let's relegate
it all to locomotive function, duplicate away—
Mucus nervosa.

Can you see without heart?

Within summary: We find our hearts.

The walls caved. (is this on)

The communal is only a service to vague, sentimental
pullings. Trappings. Each floor a turret. Worm through
the walls. A promise of poor action. A soundwave
likening. All organizational. WE COULD NEVER
LEAVE THE BODY would be a better cry.

Manifestly: The east.

I am merely, unless I'm moving, a map. Not flat. Place me in a place and I will tell you where you are regarding —

Ready for a flake? It's gemstone. Here. Here—

Time has gone away when the soreness in a neck aligns with a wall, and pulls away. When it pulls itself out, like the spirit of the little girl by the lake.

Engagement: Non-virtue.

Correlation: All my throat can ever hold.

Perhaps you should set me down in symbols. Let me take hold or suck up something.

Encourage a holding, giving, bereaving: Encourage work. Workmanship. Notation. Bringing light behind a course of me. Let me be an article of note.

Even now I remember the true embodyists. Dreamers, all of them.

As if the scroll were a coil: REWIND. Starting: Gathering under the cypresses and palms out: Hear me, he said, and then sat still for hours. Panting—shade of the cypress shifted away from the coven after many minutes— Eek cries out: But Mesu, what of your voice? And Mesu stares; enlightenment. Or, gathered and lined along a long table, to eat. The foul a seated odor. The men around Mesu begin to shout and lean against one another, but not far, and Mesu then goes: Why do you shout? And the chorale responds: Because some are angry, many are tired and few are full before this meal. And Mesu says: I am sorry for the food on the table; I am awake yesterday; I am prone to smile. And then: Enlightenment. Or when the Mesu was hung up on a wall of cane and nails were driven into him, from the sky a bird came and landed upon the dead debtor's arm, and Mesu looked down and smiled. And the guard, sword unhilted, came to cry up to him: 'You will not be smiling much longer, plight! And Mesu nods. The nails become tea. Enlightenment.

Do you feel the bubble of glory that has risen up around me? It shapes like cone, it puffs like bread. It is edible and only deep.

I have lost my temple. I have lost my tower.

Receiving?

Receiving?

Halfway through I picked a function. Imbedded in a mouth of flame. Never wrought, only through the space between teeth. Like hiding sense. Played out. A mana. Tapped, carbon soaked. The few hours devoted to meal-time and its consequence; all else is open with—

Till death do us placate. Listed as a comparable, fell a bit short. Make me use these things. Make them stop singing.

Black capacity.

Ahh! Perhaps five more sheets and I could craft a cube! A dollhouse; I'll fill it with candy. I'll fill it with finger men and finger women. I'll roll it and give them all a surprise. The house pasted together with spit and a light touch, soft as silk, soft as the mother way. Lunar and behaved. And one of the men inside the dollhouse will become a pamphleteer: Incite like the moonfull, he'll say. INCITE like the BLOODIED HAND UP!

To take the bilateral out of it: Trial, Both, Error.

Munitions supplies, an indexed average, a form that you can plug it all into. Wire hanger production and staph infections. Envelopes: Licked, stationary. Tuna belly. Races. Hunger strikes. Lacerations on the pads of the foot in the workplace. Nightly hours, everywhere. Uzi spray, average hits, all that. You can plug it all in. Then you can form another, much wider index. And that strata, now explained, will reveal itself as—

TRUMPETS, HEAVENLY LIGHT.

The hot iron ball that the saints must swallow.

I—

Limbic portends. Effervescent bouts of aphasia, twinkling necro explosions in the midrange, depth of field. Star sufferer. Compelled to shout. A curling hand, a soft and lurid odor. Not hunched, but bent. Knees in each other, grooved. Soft feet. Set to sea. The pyre lit with a remote watch, set to TIME and left, beside a gazing starfish, unspoken for, left to wash back, next to a stone, hugged undercurrent.

Or the man in bouts of smell. His fingers raw from the upnosing of them. Never far away from his hands near his nose. He did more breathing than anyone.

Balustrade: the gunmen, their knight forefathers, their mongrel widowed children.

All to avoid a hollow throat.

In the portions of one off: Do I humiliate? Should I strip back? Peel? Feel as if I never felt. Heal as if I never knew. Hung as if I never let. Shown as if I never took. Cause as if I never crawl.

Platitudes are costly, too.

Made private: Scented cloth, leather straps, flies, paste, torn (anything), erics, quail eggs, number, veins, lacri-sising, melt, ice, heaters, fiber, bread, pleasing, water, animals in heat, day bathing, venom (to the ocean) (I don't remember much)—

General intelligence, cross and well represented, corn fed, only floats in a bubble of steam. Basically miscarried. Or, a theory: There are spans inside us that take years. There are bees that make honey in winter. Hunger is a detriment, money is a seed. Juries deliberate in earnest, always. Slack is left slack because it wants a pull. Pull me. Need me?

Maladapted wingspans, too. What shifts the place of trees, what swings on dry vines. Never dropping from the tree, even under blight sun. Pleasing hands could eventually form, that too from the wingspans rearranged, a hexidecimal away. Pleasing little hands, rined in fur. See them! For it's the fruit that called a motion up, and the temple begat the city...

Milk comes through a wall.

Never: A net. I've installed them repeatedly. They all sink shut and shudder and groan.

I am! I am!

When I feel safe I think about veins.

I run lines, too; up and down the walls, or within, coming in and out, lines that intercede like eyes, lines that take something out. Too sketchy? Let me clap for you:

Now with one hand:

Past the silver bar, just under a hue of gold that ringed and took up whenever spotted. Two, beside each other. Both in spell. Nomance. After half a step of pleasure in a maze, before a full night of empty alley and the windows all silver like film. A no sight. A shouting then benched. But, before: Bar. In between a two. After a tip. Bunkered and lipping the old flame, and admissions of displeased, displaced, then to return. Admonishment. Halos. Very early ferry. Mun water. Played before on a boat, never reached, always an always but never a never. Uptaught. But, again, before: In a night of day labor he divulged his drunkest secrets.

So there's an admission to trip. You have that. On me? Like files. A cubit, shorn aside from a mother drill, looked at, really looked at, treasured. Or stolen. Or sold. Or lost. (never lost) So: Taken. Then put back into a bitmelt and made to shear again. A hesitant meld, between the two layers of impact. Like dancing amongst friends. Heat unlike—

Or the torture of drinking until the water breaks—

Gone fission—

On that lakebed. All the way at the bottom. See it? It's gold for a reason.

There will be no

Foreign bodies, or foreign entities, or foreign presences, cells, replicants, addled to memory. Those who see that all is just motion are not to be allowed, let in walls, or paid for. Let them take themselves into the desert, like births from the desert. Like a storm they can find. And a chasm when they leave, or return. Never a solid state; dank liquid.

If I played with my ears, I bet I could reach further.

Look behind you.

Waiting for a breach: Tan if washed. Been awhile since the black trolleys came through with guards.

And under what circumstances may HE become a part of the train?

Mary?

Mary?

Again: Roaming. A perpetual coastal glaze. Very hard to say.

Very hard to say.

Seems to be a different rhythm, boys. Slide up a scale. NO MUSIC—

Within the fur of the lit hand I will see the five I've pinpointed and am doomed to repeat. The strike numbers. I will see the cosmology. There are morphing stars around us, even sinking stars. A whole sky shorn in a casket and all its metals still show at you; you can see if you look close enough. It's like the grain in a photograph——

Dust?

Is a concern, yes.

The only affirmative. Make note of that; strike the records. Renege.

If you want to see outside this racket: Intimate scenes. Just see them. See them now, because you'll never see my lips on my knees again.

Once made unsure, now: Holy.
Divine growing laterally. As such I am under.
Could he return to the concern of the——

We may have to part amicably; we may have to shelf it; we may have to put it in its case; we may have to take it down, unframe it; we may have to crack it with a pin hammer and shuffle the rubble; we may have to undo the ties of the lines of instruments; we may have to dismiss the dancers; we may have to crack the disc; we may have to unplug; we may have to take off the hat, strip authority; we may have to step outside; we may have to corrupt; we may have to go outside and lose any vivid motion; we may have to take the pleasure out of the prostitution again; we may have to; we may have to refrain from talking above room tone; we may have to express ourselves only in commodity, trading posts, and sunsets avoided because the men and women, all of us, stay inside with the windows blacked.

Screed. An uneasy union between us; yes I know. Why do you think I put flowers in your hands every time we meet? You are so pretty.

Foreign tongues—well, unseen. That's what is left on you, not in smell but—there are scratches that I trace, palms cupped and suctioning out another's sweat—siphoning the past hands out of you. Again: Can't you do this on your own? Can't you do this with just one? Or another?

Again, emotive flux. Like a belly roll. An amusement, but not much outside amusement, like a slow growing tumor in a bell jar. Hesitance. Strike the likes. I can't seem to keep track of him, sir. Parsons. King.

And if I was foxhunting—

Could not gain access, so had to cut a path. PLEASE ADVISE. Urgent channels, they swell, you know. Every path has a brain.

Bled throughput. Needing. Teeth come front. Garish. Umpire. Welded cuts and their bubble blend. It's all a ruse: By now if you haven't seen—

Accusations! Hah! Perhaps we should form you a rap sheet, and start to call the items out? This is the danger in me.

I am sick and bored and want it back, the door. The hand, dark or not. I couldn't care. But the lack of everything, candidly, is forming quite a blank. And the testament I give can't hold such a rupture: The unholy blank, a middle, around it another pillow blank. These things, in accordance, are not conducive to electrical strain (me to you)—so let's play:

I'm outpacing you ten to one.

Time for the lover's tale?

Breathing.

The Fifth Difficulty: I prescribed six. You sent me into terror loops. Held a pull of uranium to my right lung.

All in accordance with the law, the law a natural extension of the hand, the hand the natural extension and body of god.

What is holiest: Speed of delivery.

There. I am sank.

There's a space in wrapping this up. But in the bubble

that the end creates, there is great urgency. Urgency like a stoked fire, or like that glint of precious metals that drives us (you god) into the earth in many ways. The ore, a stoke. A desire that even in quenching is by definition unquenched. We are born into it. Some are, some are born into a hollow chamber, much nearer to just one. I, due to spent borders, was not. Lines unknowingly employed by bipedal things, unknowingly stripped of their fundamental ambiguity. Their always. So, again: The urgency in waiting to start—FINISH—again means a great cry, a chasm with the top forced down by massive sheets of air and sound, to become a cannon, building by ricochet until burst. The canyons pop. The ears require. Birds come down to visit and salvage. The world shortens. Topped out.

I once had a longer one in me.

We could go back to the room?

Can we?

We could go back to the mocking things: Pen in my right hand, paper in my left.

We could go back to the miserly and weather, the king in exile, the mother room.

We could go back to silence.

Tempting. A sugar that never peaks and never valleys.

We could strip infinitives and talk in tone of body. Like: The wrinkles and slow beating. The crude lungs. The knees, almost broken now.

We could talk about the sense of the room.

The room.

The walls. The door. The windows. The bed. The visiting. The water. The static. The click, routinely.

Abandon: NONE OF THAT THERE—

We could leave.

It's all conversation, now, anyway. You see? Yourself at dinner, nearing the veal. Bringing in leafy greens. Smiling—said smiling. This is one possibility of I'd like to think two possibilities. The other is a non-event. The other is an alway-on button. So, to prevent the dinner:

AH—

There. I don't think—

I don't think I let that through. Maybe—

Bounce. I'll tell you: I'm bleeding and cut all over. Threw myself against the walls again. But. That's no fair. Not fun. I like gyres.

Straight slope of the nose, soft and large eyes, closed, lips that are well defined and finely cut, but lacking pout. Or glean. Cheekbones, soft, smooth, in proportion. A face in ecstasy, but a face out of sex. The safest face, swirling around the statue until it reveals itself as whatever lies under the stone. Inside the stone already, like a crystalline egg. Smooth and carved to defeat facet. What a purpose. I can see the sculptor's hands in a furry. Trace paper, the sketch, the look into the block. Look, the sketch, then stare into the block. A nimble—

Expel.

Spat it on the floor. No would be convenient, visitor. I need the light. Please. I want it for color.

I'm done.

Surface. Pain unlike a brick, but hot—a stove. All the spaces I'm leaving you, if that is what I'm leaving you, could be full of it. Full of pain. I stay plastic, but even I cannot remain neural-neutral. Call me unfashionable.

Breathing.

When the lip's gashed—dry first, then gashed—and the immediate sharp beacon becomes a lighthouse atoll, then you can run it over with your teeth, and the report back is a sigh into discomfort and an invitation into the keenest pleasure. The sharpest play. And this becomes a repeat: Teeth to lip, teeth to lip, teeth to lip. No: Not unlike the flower.

I only collect the contagious god.

I can be so much...

Oh. Oh.

I'm laughing!

Oh. This suggestion: Hunt for them. Abandon the cigarette and step back into the rain to trace the lead. Like that. That's what this suggests. So.

So.

Before I step: I am safe. Realize. What is keeping me away? No feeding—no tubes no water no brine no bristol no breathing no splurge no tack no wire no back. No hurting—no threat no invade no hit no break no slice no cut no puncture no slash no beat no arrest no burn no gag no lash no whip no shout. No fade—no take no let no bend no break no fix no let no slept no met no meet no re. No end. So in: Here. I. Am. Safe. No company.

Like promised.

Will I ever—

Mucus. Like a slug trail. That's what's leaving. I can pick up its scent and track it, down that alley. Crawling up the brick and slipping in a flush-to-wall window. The bottom of the black shoes, the khaki coat. There was a wraparound mask. Notate. Send it to the recorder, and set up the wall. Damn the rain: Make it slick. Damn the thunder: Want to hear the inside of the car, report back to recorder what clangings. Or what, if fire. So take a note. Climb up. Damned slick. Rain coming down. Remember the comic books in the brown paper sacks and their future protectors. Or not. Remember nothing. Keep blank as the brick facade leans up below you. The window is a small reach, and you almost want to stop and turn back up and reach the bottom, set out of the alleyway and go back to your car, remove the cigarette lighter, set it down on the seat beside you and go up. Let the sirens and small hats know what they missed. But you don't. You keep climbing to the window. Set so smoothly into its facade. A perfectly clean window into whatever rummaging. What the wrap-around mask is getting to up there, whether it be some document or burning by now—you have to catch it, unmask that face. Notate to recorder. Hands are reaching the edge and I can always pull myself up in a flash—that is never a problem. If the rain just—

That's an action. Were you embossed?

Is it coy if I show you what my hands are doing?

Why I spend so much time in this filthy corner, I don't know—I assure you. I know the things missed couldn't have slipped below this small dig of detritus.
The basic grace is right before you, above you.
No slash.
Moving. Next corner. This a white and almost jellied. Understand where it all should've been—not in a certain color or mood but in a pulse. Like pulling up instead of

pulling down, esophageal. The mirror of stomach and uterus. That's a pop psych. Now that's a fiction!

Nothing here. My hands are gloves.

So many steps before the next corner. A clever map that I haven't drawn yet—oh well. Here now. Messing. This air is so nope! Nothing.

Trek. Should I even begin to describe the fourth? Or is it better to leave it a line, and let you zoom in on a point and point on as I go—

I'm left with all this land before me! The mountainous planes! The hilled valleys! Roaming on the grass and snow feels so good, and the better breathing. This is the healthiest thing I've ever done.

The confession to the mother about the selfsame event of last year. Not an adventure.

So, in failing, I'm left with all the rest. The all but corners. The sap bottom of a deep well. The place just below the grifted machines in their upwards sucking; the sound around a consonant. Pourous blood, or shale. Quaked salt. (me!) If I set off now, the safari will not be far behind. A jungle in creeping. Vines a—

Start. Move foot next. The dirt below like a catching or great handshake between fault lines. Sacrament because of the day in which all the people saw the worlds laid out in traps before them, ripe shining traps full of all the world's starting points. I vow to never X an X again.

That old age is a constant haven-forward stooping. Born again is the trailer before the movie.

Am I inducing anger? Am I making anger? Loam.

The romantics disavow the Word—strike it from their dictionaries and burn inscribed plates, their soft pillows, clothes, notebooks, devices. They burn each other in somas. The Word is kept for later. (keep peeking!)

Eternity is the combustion engine.

Some see the two oldest dancers as assassin and political figure—always sculpting the other's legacy and circling in theatres.

Could I just look up again?

...

In amber.

I am the beggar that chooses.

Look again. You'll grow a new leaf.

What I really see is this room amid a big fire, kept from the heat but deep in the river of it, caught in its current but unmoving. A set stone. I see this with stars in my eyes.

I have gone awhile. My longest. You are still in the pews but the crosslight behind me is dimming. A timer clicks.

I have feet to scan over, hands to run and a tongue to work—won't show you the tongue but the hands and feet are calloused and don't breathe past that certain skin.

Great gaps, deepening chasms, going slightly deeper per minute than the falling all of us.

In hoping you are left to muck with the gathered light,
on the floor:

Two lovers. Sleeping in bed. Asleep for hours. Their eyes faintly twitch, a dance to anyone who would watch. One begins to mutter, lips part a bit and the throat makes a low sound. Then a word. A word belonging to its own axis, and still spinning with its company. So one lover speaks. A parable in dream. The other lover wakes. The noise is too much to ignore and sleep deeply through. The other lover watches the speaking mouth, and listens and means to remember this speech and its odd and tilting way, to recite back this speech to the speaking lover when they are both awake. The dream speech slows, becomes intermittent, then winds off in murmur. The listening lover falls asleep before the last word is spoken, and is taken into a deeper and more imaginative sleep. The listening lover, now sleeping, begins to murmur too, at a rapid pace, and the words build on each other to form strings of melting things, until the pace is strong enough to hold steady as the sleeping lover now goes louder, talking almost conversationally, amid an action somewhere deep and hidden, enough to wake the other lover who immediately notes the urgency of this speech, then its lilt, then its belonging to a dream, then its nuances, its steady and shifting rhythm, and notes to remember this, pick up certain phrases to hold until morning when the other lover can listen to this odd soliloquy that they can talk about together, this speech in sleep of all places, so the newly listening lover happily falls back asleep in front of a track of talk that eventually, minutes later, slows and ceases. The newly sleeping lover enters a span of sleep that goes out wide on all sides and doesn't seem to stop, and feels a strange current, and in sleep begins to speak in fervor, a warbling diluted appeal to some one thing above all of it, and the other lover wakes again and is taken so strongly by the passion, this speech, that, newly awake and determined to remember this, for this is strong enough to always be unfamiliar, the listening lover forgets the prior waking and listens intently, pushing back sleep in spurs that go in and fade and go in and fade like the errant way of talking in which the other lover still speaks, still speaking, but the wave is too under cut by sleep, and sleep pulls the listening lover back, while the other lover continues for awhile and then comes to rest again. And just as the last listening lover is gripped again and let roam in something wild—

No. Too easy.

(who knows)

(where is who)

Whither.

Bereft of space and gone of place there is nothing to hold. Infantile names. Supposition. Quiet faith is great parricide.

I am the problem that vanishes.

(bow, fall back, into smoke)